THE
ADVENTURES
OF
JAMIL

MOHAMMED UMAR

Salaam Publishing

LONDON

First published in the United Kingdom in 2012 by
Salaam Publishing, 72 Ivy Road, London, NW2 6SX, UK
salaampublishing@gmail.com

ISBN   978-0-9572084-0-7

Design and cover illustration by Judith Charlton
www.judithcharlton.co.uk

Contents

Author's Note

This story was not meant to be written. The idea that kicked it off was a simple one. In April 2004 I told my daughter Nafisa a one-off bedtime story of a boy who fulfilled his dream by leaving the mountain and going down to the valley. It was a simple adventure story for a child. The next day and to my utmost surprise Nafisa remembered the story and wanted to know what eventually happened to the boy. I was forced to continue the story because her brothers, Salim and Karim, were also interested in it. With the active participation of all three, the story developed and the boy was named Jamil. When the story took a particular shape they encouraged me to write it down and get it published.

The more I thought about the story the more ideas came and, as often happens, a whole new world opened up before me. Characters, places and incidents suggested themselves and dictated the nature of the evolving story. Inevitably the story I eventually wrote in February 2010 was different from the story of 2004. Just like my children the story had grown from a children's story to a story for teenagers.

I've deliberately structured the story so that it begins near the end, reaches the end and then starts at the beginning and works its way to the middle. Then it gets to the end which is not really the end because it comes back to the beginning which in reality is near the end! There are no places that I know of called Tatasi Peninsula, Pashia Kingdom or Pearl Islands. All names of characters, places and incidents in this story are fictional and thus any resemblance to living or dead persons, to places, to past, present and future events are purely accidental. I thank Nafisa, Karim and Salim for the inspiration. I also want to thank Berthe van Mansvelt (*in loving memory*) and Friso van Mansvelt for providing the perfect conditions for the inspiration to thrive.

August 2011
Chalet Marysa, Gryon, Switzerland

For my late mother Halima for everything

'The bold adventurer succeeds the best.'
Ovid

CHAPTER ONE

Return to Pearl Islands

It was early evening. The sun was casting a light reddish glow on the Pearl Islands as the plane approached Massa International Airport.

Jamil sat quietly by the window seat looking out expectantly. So many things were going through his mind. 'What will the island look like? Will I be able to recognise anything given the long absence? Will I be able to find my relatives and friends?' Jamil looked through the window and saw dotted clouds and the sun setting in the distance.

'*Cabin crew prepare for landing*,' the pilot's voice disturbed his thoughts.

Jamil took a deep breath. It finally dawned on him that he would be landing in his homeland in a matter of minutes. It was a place he had left nineteen years ago in search of the golden key.

'Home at last,' whispered Haske who was sitting next to him, 'and with the key.' She was excited. She smiled at him, took a deep breath and started to tie her huge curly hair. When she had finished, Haske tapped him gently on his thigh. 'Everything will be fine,' she reassured him. Her eyes were as sparkling as ever with joy and excitement. 'Okay, fasten your seatbelt,' she said smiling. He fastened the belt but remained silent.

The plane descended and landed.

Jamil's curious eyes could not see anything familiar from the plane. The airport was built on an artificial island far out in the sea; faraway from the island he used to live on. He tried to picture what the island would look like but could not.

'Everything will be fine,' Haske said as they stepped out of the plane.

'Do you have anything to declare?' asked a Customs officer looking at Jamil.

'No,' Jamil answered politely.

'Open your bag for inspection please,' the officer demanded.

Jamil opened as requested.

'What is this?' the same officer asked, pointing at a partly wrapped item in Jamil's rucksack.

'It's a souvenir from Pashia Kingdom,' Jamil replied.

'But what is it?' the officer persisted.

'It is part of a key ... an antique,' Jamil explained.

'I see. You can go,' the officer waved.

Jamil and Haske walked into the arrival hall where they were greeted by a huge sign: WELCOME TO PEARL ISLANDS – *Where the Sun Never Sets!* Jamil felt strange as they walked slowly through the hall. Nothing around him was familiar. Wherever he looked, he saw shops and boutiques.

'And this airport was built in the sea?' he asked no one in particular.

'Yes, Jamil, it's on an artificial island,' Haske volunteered an answer.

'Incredible,' said a bewildered Jamil.

The two walked to the information desk where a young lady in red and white uniform welcomed them with a broad smile. 'Welcome to Pearl Islands, the land of prosperity as some of us call it,' the lady said still smiling. 'How can I help you?'

'How can we get to Gariyon?' Jamil asked.

'Old or New Gariyon?' the lady asked.

Jamil looked at Haske as if she had the answer written on her face. Haske smiled. The young lady at the counter explained. 'The old Gariyon is in Jaycity which is on the main island called Grand Massa Island. The new Gariyon is very far away in a place called Newfoundland.'

'I'm confused,' Jamil confessed.

'The new Gariyon is definitely not a place for tourists like you. It's a ghetto far beyond the mountains. Whereas the old Gariyon is for visitors like you. There is more life there than in the new one. There are more things to see and relate to there. There are discos, shops, hotels, banks, casinos.'

'Where are the inhabitants of the old Gariyon?' Jamil asked.

'They were all relocated to the new Gariyon about a decade ago to make room for modernisation and redevelopment.'

'I see,' Jamil said nodding his head.

'I would recommend you go to the old Gariyon because that's where the fun is. There's nothing in the new Gariyon for people to see and to be honest it can be dangerous at times.'

'How do we get there?' Haske asked. 'I can't wait to have fun.'

'You could either go by boat from Exit One or take the undersea train from Exit Two. They both go to Villancia. From there you take bus number 10 which terminates at Jaycity,' the lady explained whilst looking at a map of the Pearl Islands.

'You mean there is a train service under the sea?' a perplexed Jamil asked.

'Yes, Massa Metro runs from the airport to Grand Massa Island every ten minutes, under the sea,' the lady explained.

'That's incredible.' Jamil stared at the lines and colours of the map. The lady noticed and explained.

'We've seven islands. Two are natural islands and five are artificial islands, including the one we are standing on right now.'

'I see,' Jamil said not fully understanding what she meant. 'Tell me something. How did the name Pearl Islands come about?'

'After the Twin Tragedy – that's the devastating earthquake and volcanic eruption that took place about twenty years ago, the Tatasi Peninsula was destroyed. Just when all hope was lost, pearls were discovered and in huge quantities too.'

'What do you mean by all hope lost?'

'After the Twin Tragedy, nothing could grow on the new island. Not even the plant called Tatasi that made the place rich and famous.'

'Where do you get your food from?' Haske asked.

'Everything is imported.'

'Everything?'

'We're rich enough to import everything.'

'What about fish? I like fish a lot,' Haske asked excitedly.

'As you'll see there is very little room for fish farms and

economically it works better to import than to fish in the waters around here.'

'Let me get this right,' Jamil said looking seriously at her. 'What you are saying is that there are no more Tatasi farms on Tatasi Island.'

'Sorry sir, no more Tatasi plants on Pearl Islands. However, there are some plants in the Tatasi museum for tourists like you to see and touch,' she said smiling. Jamil was not offended at being called a tourist.

'Thank you very much,' Jamil said.

'Enjoy your stay.'

Jamil and Haske decided to take the boat to Villancia. The view across the sea for Jamil was eye popping. From the deck, he could see a panorama of bridges, water, endless skyscrapers. 'This is incredible,' he exclaimed as the boat headed towards Grand Massa Island. What caught Jamil's eyes most were the skyscrapers and tower blocks competing for space in the sky. Some had scaffolding.

From Villancia Jamil and Haske took bus number 10 which crossed a big bridge and went through overpasses and tunnels towards what he took to be the centre of Grand Massa Island. Jamil was visibly overwhelmed. 'This is amazing. I didn't expect this at all.'

'Can you differentiate between the houses built on the main island and the ones on artificial islands?' Haske asked as they rode on the bus.

'No,' Jamil answered with his mouth still wide open. 'Look, there are even houses with golden domes. We never had them before.'

Jamil and Haske alighted at Massa square; three stops from Jaycity. He wanted to walk the rest of the journey. The square was teeming with tourists taking pictures of a statue in the middle of the square. He was not interested in that, but was struggling to get his bearings. A few things began to make sense.

'Yes,' he said with excitement. 'The House of Samad used to be there where the statue is standing. The lighthouse used to be there but it's no more or it's covered by these skyscrapers.' He paused. 'Now I know exactly where we are,' he said, leading Haske towards old Gariyon. They walked past a sprawling complex of luxurious villas. One had Babulosa Exotic Village written on the gates.

'Things have really changed,' he blurted out.

'What do you mean?' Haske asked.

'Almost everything has changed,' Jamil emphasised.

'But that's what happens when…'

'No. Not the buildings.'

'Then what?' asked Haske.

Jamil thought for a while and responded. 'Something is missing. I can feel it already. I knew that the new people on the island would be different but I've noticed something that disturbs me. The people are not close to each other. They are not connected to each other anymore. Something is definitely missing … maybe it's me not connected to the island anymore.'

'It's not you Jamil. I see what you mean. We're in a crowd but not with them. Maybe when we go to Newfoundland we'll feel part of them,' agreed Haske.

'Maybe! Look at the faces of these people. They are like a gallery of pictures with something missing in their eyes.'

'I see. The people hardly speak to each other.'

'Look at how they walk like zombies.'

'There seems to be something wrapped around each individual … something invisible,' said Haske.

'This was exactly the opposite of life on the island before I left. Then people were accessible. You could talk to people freely and could see there was life in them. Then there was warmth and love. The people smiled a lot – genuine smiles and laughter that came from the heart, as we used to say. Before I left, the people took time to sit or stand and have a good conversation. I knew I'd face a form of loneliness after all these years away but I wasn't prepared for this,' said a dejected Jamil.

Haske did not reply. She left him to his thoughts. They continued walking.

Jamil could not help but notice that there were so many banks with different names. He also noticed that there were no customers in them. He briefly wondered what attracted all these banks and financial institutions to his beloved island. He also noticed many expensive shops and boutiques. There were rows of shops but few customers in them too. It was not what was bothering him now.

'Haske,' Jamil started with a smile. 'Look, there,' he pointed at a shopping mall, 'was where we had a small farm of Tatasi ... and there,' he pointed at a ten storey building that had PRESIDENTIAL HOTEL on it, 'was where I rescued Lucky, my pet goat.' As they walked along slowly he showed her more places. 'I used to play football with Bashir and other kids there ... where you have the multistorey car park. Yes, my school. Can you see that shopping centre there with huge antennas at the top?'

'Yes.'

'That was where our school was. The casino there was where we used to rest and practice our songs and parades ... and see that building there?

'Which one? The one with MASSA INTERNATIONAL BANK?'

'Yes, that was where the monster devoured Lucky.' He paused. 'This whole place,' he said pointing to skyscrapers with window-less walls, 'was just a vast land for us to play, wander and hunt in.'

As they continued their walk, Jamil glimpsed a house hidden behind a tall building that resembled his grandfather's home. Jamil shouted with excitement with his two hands in the air. 'Look, that's my grandparent's house! The house my grandfather Kamal and his friend Uncle Majid built with their hands,' he said with a sense of pride in his deep voice, and pointing at a wooden bungalow. As they approached it he noticed it was fenced and there was a guard at the gate. It looked better maintained than it was when he left.

'Excuse me please, what is this house?' Jamil asked the guard.

'It's a museum,' the guard answered.

'What sort of museum?'

'Can't you see it's different from all houses around here?' the guard asked indifferently.

'That's why I'm asking.'

'There is a noticeboard there that explains what it is,' the guard said pointing at a board a few metres away. 'It's one of the only houses that survived the earthquake intact. So it is preserved for posterity as it represents the architecture of that period. It's actually the only house of that period on the islands.'

'Can we go in?' Haske asked.

'Of course not. It's state property and you need a special permission from the authorities,' the guard replied.

'Where can we get the permission?' Jamil asked.

'From the municipality office of CVD in New Harlem.'

'But he was born and brought up in the house,' Haske intervened in defence of Jamil.

'That's none of my business,' the guard said and walked away.

'My grandmother used to sit there, on that bench. That was her favourite place. She always liked sitting facing the setting sun. There are a few Tatasi plants in the courtyard as you can see. My catapult and wooden key are probably in there where I left them almost nineteen years ago.'

'Amazing isn't it? I'm really happy for you that the house is still standing. I hope we'll one day go inside,' Haske said looking at Jamil who seemed to have been transfixed to the spot. He looked at the house and at Haske but could not utter a single word. 'Life is like that. These things do happen,' she said pulling him away. 'Now show me where you tricked the monster,' she said getting excited. Jamil led her towards the new harbour.

'At least one thing has not changed,' Jamil said with a smile.

'What's that?'

'Look,' he said, pointing at a triangular shaped formation of white birds flying in the sky. 'We called them *Leke-Leke* and strongly believed they brought the rains. They always flew over before the rains.' Jamil laughed. 'Even in dry seasons we still begged them for rains.'

'I'm thirsty,' Haske said when the reached the harbour.

'Okay, let's have a drink first,' Jamil suggested and they walked into a café.

As they sat and drank in silence, a yacht filled with lightly-dressed men and women sped into the harbour. They were all laughing. The skipper pressed the horn twice for no reason. 'Don't mind him,' the bar attendant said. 'Everyone shows off here.' Jamil looked around in disgust at the display of such wealth. 'It's new and the owner wants everybody to notice him. Don't pay any attention. There'll be a parade next month and then you'll see really big and expensive yachts. This entire place will be full and there'll be all-night parties on them too. If you have time come and watch.'

'What's the name of this area now?' asked an intrigued Jamil.

'It's got two names. Some people call it Gold Coast because rich people all over the world deposit their money in the banks here, while others call it Millionaire's Playground,' the bar attendant explained.

When they were ready Jamil led Haske down to the water's edge. 'This place used to be the closest point to the mainland and that was why I chose to cross from this point.' Jamil's voice was barely audible. He paused. 'There,' pointing at where a huge white yacht was marooned, 'was where I released the first goat-in-the-boat.' He paused. He felt as if something blocked his throat. He felt dizzy. 'And there,' he continued, pointing to where a party yacht was about to leave, 'was where I released the second goat-in-the-boat.' Jamil paused again. His voice cracked. 'And here,' he broke down in tears, 'here, where this yacht is,' pointing at another party boat right in front of them, 'was where I released the third goat-in-the-boat and dived into the waters that early morning all those years ago.'

Haske comforted him. 'You did what you were supposed to do.'

'Indeed,' Jamil answered thoughtfully, as they walked past open bars, restaurants, new luxury resorts and gated mansions. It was getting dark but there was light everywhere. There were people walking and working everywhere, unlike before he left when people were all resting and waiting to go to bed around this time. Now he understood why they were also called THE ISLANDS THAT NEVER SLEEP!

The next day Haske asked Jamil, 'When are we going to Newfoundland? I'm eager to meet the real Tatasians.'

'Maybe in a day or two.'

'Why are you not in a hurry to meet your people?' she pressed further.

'Why should I? I've been away for such a long time and no one is expecting me anyway,' Jamil responded with a shrug.

'Okay, where are we going to today?' Haske asked smiling.

'To a place that was called Baritaye but is now called New Harlem.'

'Why New Harlem?'

'I've no idea. I'm a tourist in my homeland,' he joked.

In New Harlem, Jamil did not bother to ask why there was a change of name. He was beginning to accept the changes and that he was not part of the new island anymore. He was beginning to accept that things had moved on and he must too. Jamil noticed there were large scale redevelopments taking place. The main attraction was the new palace that was being built. It was a replica of the old one that was destroyed during the earthquake twenty years ago. Jamil took Haske to the Tatasi museum and explained in detail all its uses and how important it was to the people of the peninsula before the Twin Tragedy. 'I always wanted to be a Tatasi farmer like my grandfather,' Jamil said as they walked out of the museum. They returned to the preserved parts of Grand Massa Island in Jaycity. It was teeming with tourists who wandered through the maze of ruins, streets and cafes. As they went through the ruins of a particular building, Jamil looked at Haske. 'It's as if the ruins are talking to me.'

Jamil and Haske continued to explore the area. They walked in Massa square and drifted towards Massa statue. Jamil was not initially interested but decided to look at the statue closely. It was neither human nor a recognisable animal. It had three different faces, each a different colour, and each looking in three different directions. As he stood there wondering what it was, Haske stepped closer. 'What is this statue?'

'I don't know. It says here *Saviour of the Tatasi Island.*'

'Very strange and weird looking statue,' Haske commented. 'Who is Massa?'

'I don't know. But look, someone is about to explain what it is to a group of foreign tourists.'

The two joined the group who had gathered in front of the statue. A tour guide holding a loudspeaker explained:

'As you all know, twenty years ago next week a devastating earthquake struck one fateful night and destroyed more than half this main island. Actually it was a peninsula and the earthquake turned it into an island. It was believed that the strip of land that attached it to the mainland held it afloat, and that the new island would have sunk into the sea killing everyone were it not for a monster that rose from the depths of the sea just in time to keep the island afloat.

'The monster was so powerful that it was able to stop further earthquakes and it even produced a volcanic eruption that created another island nearby. The new island formed by the monster helped keep the main island steady and when the monster attached them together they both became stable. The monster blew away a particular cloud that settled over the new island. The monster raised the island in some parts and actually pushed the new island closer to the mainland. That's how powerful it was.

'The monster protected the two islands and the inhabitants from further disasters. So in other words, these two islands survived thanks to the extraordinary powers of the monster. When the monster realised its time was up, it released its grip on the islands and died a natural and honourable death. The demise of the monster led directly to our prosperity because the monster decomposed and turned into pearls – abundant and high quality pearls, which are our main export today.

'In appreciation of all it has done, we don't want to call it a monster as it was called immediately after the Twin Tragedy, we call it Master – master of our destiny. The original inhabitants of this island – the Tatasians – could not pronounce Master, they said Massa. That's why we have Massa International Airport, Grand

Massa Avenue, Massa Plaza, Massa Park, Massa Metro, Massa University and Massa Bay. We are all standing on Massa Square in front of Massa Statue.

'The statue is made of bronze and has three different faces because no one ever saw the face of the monster. It was very shy. The three faces thus represent the past, present and future of the islands. If you look at the Coat-of-Arms of Pearl Islands, you'll see a face of the monster with the words: *Courage, Unity and Prosperity*. We have different faces of the monster on our currencies. The monster loved the Tatasians. Massa means everything to us.'

'Long live Massa!' the tour guide shouted and bowed to the statue.

'Long live Massa!' the tourists responded and bowed to the statue.

Jamil and Haske did not join the chorus and did not bow to the statue. They looked at each other in disbelief. She flashed her sympathetic smile again. 'This is incredible,' Jamil was forced to say shaking his head. 'I cannot believe what I've just heard. How could they change the history of the island like this?'

Haske dragged him away from the statue. 'Don't worry Jamil. As Queen Natasha used to say, truth has a funny way of coming out, sometimes when one least expects it. The truth will one day come out, like the sun and the moon. One day the world will know the truth.'

CHAPTER TWO

Jamil the Saviour

From their sixth floor room at Grand Massa Hotel Jamil's saddened face looked down at the square. He stood there confused and angry. What he and Haske had heard earlier disturbed him. From where he was standing, he could see hundreds of tourists walking on Massa Square and around Massa Statue. 'Look at these people!' his deep voice shook the room. 'Look at them, bowing to the statue of the monster day and night.' Haske joined him by the window. Photography flashed across the well-lit Massa square. From their room, they could hear the shouts of 'Long Live Massa! Long Live Massa!'

'There's even a Massa Museum where people can see the stuffed Massa and pay homage,' he said showing Haske a leaflet. 'See this one,' Jamil said with a grimace. 'There will be week-long celebrations to mark two important dates next week – the day Massa saved the island and Massa Remembrance Day.'

'I don't understand.'

After a pause, Jamil explained to Haske: 'It'll be exactly twenty years next week since the Twin Tragedy occurred and exactly nineteen years ago when I carried out my three-goat-plan and embarked on my adventure.' The disappointment was clear on Jamil's face.

Haske, who until now had been very strong and positive had joined him in a state of hopelessness. 'You mean we went through all that to get to this point? This is simply unbelievable. This is not real. Just tell me somehow that I'm dreaming,' Haske said, bringing out the golden key from Jamil's bag and putting it on the bed. 'What are we going to do now?'

'I don't know,' Jamil said absentmindedly. After their experiences that day, Jamil was beginning to ask himself whether it had been a good idea to return to the island in the first place. 'We should have just remained in Rasmarat. It'd have been better to have the island in my memory than come back to this.' Jamil had been so proud of what he did for the island and although he never expected to be rewarded, he didn't expect such changes. 'I don't belong to this place anymore,' he said shaking his head sadly. 'I'm a stranger on my island. Luckily I didn't die while fighting for the key ...'

'It would have been a waste.'

'But I really enjoyed fighting the chimeras,' he said smiling for the first time that evening. 'Somehow my instinct told me that the key would be useless in the new environment ... but it was fun getting it. As the old man in the Land of Mourners said: It's the journey to get the key that matters. I've learnt a lot and those experiences are not a waste. Were it not for the search for the key, I wouldn't have met you and we wouldn't be here today ...'

'... and happy together,' Haske added with a smile.

'You're right,' Jamil said walking closer to Haske, 'I suggest we go to Newfoundland tomorrow afternoon. This is not a place for us.'

Haske looked at him and at the square below. 'I don't think I'll believe anything I hear on this island and I think we'll be at home with the original inhabitants, the Tatasians.'

'Okay, I agree with you.'

'I really look forward to meeting your relatives and friends. I think we can relate to them and they'll understand the significance of the key,' said Haske.

'These people don't know anything about the key and don't need it. They have the monster.'

'... And we have the key.'

The next morning the two packed their bags and were ready to go to Newfoundland in the afternoon after taking a walk on Massa Square again. 'I read in a leaflet that there is an ultra-modern shopping centre right underneath the square. Maybe we should just see what it looks like before we proceed to Newfoundland,' Haske suggested.

'Okay. We have the time.'

As they walked Jamil noticed that the sun was not really felt on the streets as it used to be when he was younger. He thought it was blocked by the tall buildings. It was not the sunlight and brightness he used to love and appreciate. Later, Jamil asked Haske, 'Do you notice how strangely people are behaving today?'

'You always notice strange things. You expect them to do exactly what they did over twenty years ago?' Haske said, somewhat irritated.

'No,' he said intently. 'Look. See how they are all glued to TV screens.'

'There must be something interesting like football, the lottery or something.'

Jamil felt there was more to it than that and approached a group of people in a café. 'Good morning. What's going on, if I may ask?'

'A huge earthquake is expected very soon,' a man replied with fear in his eyes.

'Where?'

'Here of course. Where else?'

'I don't understand,' Jamil pressed further.

'Scientists are predicting another huge earthquake here very soon, maybe within days. Do you understand now? Go and buy the newspapers or pay to watch the news.'

'Thanks,' Haske said pulling Jamil away nervously. They bought *Massa Truth*, *Pearl Daily*, *Grand Massa News*.

Jamil read the highlights to Haske:

'A team of world scientists have concluded a decade-long research on the geology of the Pearl Islands;

'Scientists are sure that there'll be a huge earthquake around the islands soon but have not ruled out the possibility of a series of powerful earthquakes – in a matter of days!;

'Scientists have found the fault line that runs under the islands. The epicentre of the big earthquake is off Grand Massa Island and could produce a twenty metre tidal wave that could wipe out everything on the islands;

'All islands must be evacuated immediately;

'Scientists believe that the old golden key is the only thing that can save the islands;

'Half of the golden key is on the island;

'The race is on to find the other half but no one on the island has any idea where to look for it.

Jamil and Haske looked at each other in disbelief.

'This is unbelievable,' exclaimed Haske. 'My grandmother might be right after all.'

'Yes, Hakuri might be right,' Jamil said calmly nodding his head. 'Yesterday we thought the key was useless ...'

'And now it's the hottest thing to have.'

'Things don't just happen,' Jamil said smiling.

'Will you give them the key?'

'Of course,' Jamil said without any hesitation. 'As your grandmother used to say, just when you want strange things to happen, they do happen.'

Haske was visibly excited. 'Now you know why she called you Ming; the person born under the lucky stars. The adventurer who successfully reached his destination.'

They ran out of the building when the fire alarm went off. Loudspeakers were also blaring messages: "Evacuate the Pearl Islands. You have twenty-four hours to evacuate the islands."

'I suggest you go to the World Scientific Research Centre immediately. It's just round the corner,' said a hotel staff member when Jamil confided that he might know where the other half of the golden key was. The two raced to the building which was the tallest building on the street. Jamil was pleasantly surprised when he saw a huge sign: WELCOME TO THE TOWER OF SAMAD.

Jamil had difficulty explaining to the security guard that he knew where the other half of the key was. After a long argument, Jamil approached a man he guessed was the director as he walked with aides through the door of the building.

'My name is Jamil and I'd like to talk to you about the other half of the golden key.'

'You indeed look like a Tatasian; your height, deep voice and your manners,' the man said and asked Jamil to follow him. After taking a few steps, the man stopped, looked closely at Jamil and whispered. 'You mean the Jamil that tricked the monster nineteen years ago?'

'Yes' Jamil replied in a low voice nodding his head.

'Welcome back,' the man said smiling.

On the twenty-fifth floor, the director explained: 'All the buildings on Pearl Islands are designed to withstand an earthquake of about 8.0 on the Richter scale. What we are expecting in the next twenty-four hours or so is going to be a lot stronger, somewhere around 10.0 or more on the Richter scale. Yes, we're expecting the big one.'

'Are you expecting one or more earthquakes?' Haske asked.

'We are sure of the *big one*, but our data points to more than one. We could have multiple powerful earthquakes at the same time. One on the island and another in the sea.'

'Why are you looking for the old key?' Jamil asked.

'What can it do?' Haske pressed further.

'Scientists have been able to put sensors deep into the earth and can now monitor seismic activities. We've been able to dig huge valves all around the islands to release the pressure that causes the plates to hit each other, which as you know causes earthquakes. In this process we found out that the only way we can stop further earthquakes is by releasing the heat, which can only be done by using the old golden key.'

'The Gift from the Heavens,' said Jamil.

'Yes, that's what it was called years ago.'

'What about the key in the encased golden box,' Jamil asked.

'How do you know about that?' the director asked with a smile.

'I was a member of the Guardian of the Key Brigade years ago and we used to carry it around.'

'I said you look like a real Tatasian! The key you carried around was fake and as such cannot do the job.'

'Why can't scientists make a new key?'

'We've tried every trick under the sun but nothing worked. The only thing that shows signs that it'll work is when we use our half of the old golden key. So our belief is that when the two are fixed together it will work.'

'Can you explain to me what is going on?' Haske pleaded. 'I'm scared. I don't want to die here.'

The director took them to a computer with a huge screen. He clicked the mouse and showed them live pictures from beneath the Grand Massa Island and the sea. 'As you can see these are live pictures showing how the plates are moving closer.'

'I'm scared,' Haske cried.

'It's not immediate, okay?' Jamil calmed her down.

'What if it happens now? Jamil we're on the twenty-fifth floor. I'm terrified.'

'We'll be fine, don't worry.'

The director clicked the mouse and continued. 'These are indicators. Should they turn red, there'll be an earthquake. As you can see, it's orange but it can change any time and based on our recent observations, it'll turn red within the next twenty-four hours or so.'

'Jamil, I don't want to die here, okay?' Haske was getting nervous.

'Haske, we've enough time to get out of this place or sort things out.'

The director clicked and showed a computer simulation of how the key would help release the pressure and avert a catastrophe. 'As you can see with the right key, there'll be no more earthquakes here again because we can release the pressure from underneath the earth whenever it builds up from here,' he pointed to a hole in the wall next to the computers.

Jamil found it hard to believe. 'As you can see the situation is critical,' said the director. 'We desperately need the other half of the key to save the islands and everything on them.'

'What about Newfoundland, is it safe there?'

'Yes,' said the Director. 'The mountain range between the islands and Newfoundland will absorb the pressure and prevent any tsunami overwhelming the settlements there.'

'I told you let's go to Newfoundland. I don't trust these machines and cannot believe any story I hear on this island,' Haske said.

'Calm down, Haske,' Jamil pleaded.

'What if it doesn't work?' Haske queried.

'We'll survive somehow. I survived the first one and we'll survive this one,' Jamil assured her with a big smile.

'The key will work,' the director added looking at Haske. 'We're positive.'

'Thanks for taking us through this, especially when time is so short,' Jamil said calmly. 'I'm pleased to inform you that I can get the other half of the key. I know where it is. I'll bring it here in two hours time.' Jamil did not want to give it to him immediately. He wanted time to think it through.

Jamil told the director how he had survived the first earthquake twenty years ago. How he had tricked and killed the monster, travelled to many places and brought back the key only a couple of days ago.

'Just in time,' the joyous director said. 'We knew about you, the old key and its importance, but our history has been rewritten so much that the real things became myths while the monster is now glorified.'

'I'll see you in two hours time.'

'I'll be downstairs waiting.'

The two shook hands firmly.

Exactly two hours later Jamil and Haske were shown on live television as they approached the Tower of Samad. As they walked towards the building, TV cameras focused on Jamil as he held his rucksack tightly. They walked calmly, Haske smiling at Jamil who was visibly nervous. 'Everything will be okay,' she whispered as they approached the steps of the building.

A TV journalist stepped forward: 'Jamil, how do you feel about holding the key to the future of the Pearl Islands?'

'No comment.'

'It must be a huge responsibility,' the journalist continued.

'No comment.'

'Is it true you had to cross the desert and even fight chimeras to get it?'

'Yes.'

'Do you know that what is in your rucksack could validate a new scientific theory in the way earthquakes are prevented?'

'No comment.'

'Should the key work, the history of the islands will have to be rewritten.'

'Let's hope it works.'

'Is there anything you'd like to say?'

'I want to thank Haske for her support.'

On the twenty-fifth floor of the Tower of Samad, Jamil calmly opened his rucksack in the full glare of television cameras and handed the key to the director who kissed it and handed it to a team of five scientists. They examined, measured and weighed the key. They nodded in agreement with each other. They walked to where the other half was and fixed them together. As soon as it clicked there was jubilation among the scientists.

'Wow! It's the right key,' screamed the TV commentator reporting live from the twenty-fifth floor of the Tower of Samad. The scientists invited Jamil to step forward and insert the key into a hole.

'Can Haske help me?'

'Of course,' said the director. 'She played a very important role in getting the key.'

Jamil and Haske inserted the key slowly and turned it under the instructions of the scientists. As they turned the key slowly, they were told that gas was coming out of the twelve huge valves around the islands. The director kept his eyes on the computer screen and reported to other scientists:

'Pressure easing! Pressure easing! Plates normal, plates normal. Green colour change. Green colour change. All Valves in operation.'

About thirty minutes later the director announced: 'The seismometer is showing that things are back to normal. The key has worked. The Pearl Islands have been saved.' The team of scientists hugged and thanked Jamil and Haske.

'The big one has been averted. What an escape!' the director said hugging Jamil. 'You've saved everybody and everything on the Pearl Islands. You are our saviour.'

CHAPTER THREE

In The Beginning

One early morning, Jamil woke up to the first signs of life on Tatasi Peninsula. As he opened his eyes, he smiled. He was excited because Uncle Majid would be visiting the family today. Jamil knew Uncle Majid would bring a present for him. He always did whenever he visited. Last year, Uncle Majid had given Jamil a hand-woven multicoloured hat. Jamil proudly wore it around as it was unique on the peninsula.

Jamil could hear the familiar early morning bird songs. He had got so used to their songs that he knew what time it was from which bird was singing. It was as if there was a queue of birds singing one after the other. When it got to a particular birdsong, Jamil knew it was time to get up. On this particular day, he got up before the bird even started singing. He got ready to accompany his grandfather Kamal for his early morning dip, something he had done ever since he could walk the distance. Jamil and his grandfather usually walked in the early morning darkness to what was popularly known as the Magic Pass – a strip of land that connected the mainland to the peninsula.

Kamal usually stepped out of the wooden house first. Jamil followed obediently. Jamil loved the routine – how he would wake up, imitate the way his grandfather stretched his body, dressed, prayed and even how he always stepped out of the house with his right leg. Jamil would imitate his grandfather's recitations of verses that sought the protection of his family and property in his absence. 'May my steps lead me to the right path.' The walk to the Magical Pass in the early morning darkness was usually silent. On this particular day, Kamal broke the silence. 'You're too fast for me. Please slow down.' Jamil slowed down and walked behind the old man.

'What time is Uncle Majid coming?' Jamil asked, not for the first time.

'In the afternoon,' Kamal answered.

'Can I come with you to the port?'

'Of course.'

There was no further conversation until they reached the Magic Pass. The old man took his time as he always did. He tested the water, first with his right hand and then with his right foot. Then he said a prayer before diving into the sea. He swam slowly far out into the sea until Jamil lost sight of him in the morning darkness. Normally Jamil would wander around until he heard the splashes close to the pass then he would return to where his grandfather usually put his clothes. On this particular day, Jamil did not wander around. He sat next to his grandfather's clothes and watched Kamal swim back to the pass with admiration and respect. He loved his grandfather. Jamil was five years old when his parents moved out of the family house to the Baritaye part of the peninsula. They left Jamil with his grandparents because they both worked and had little time to bring him up. He was the first and only grandchild and his grandparents adored him.

By now the sun was rising slowly.

'A daily dip is essential,' said Kamal who was emphatic about the health-giving properties of the sea. 'It makes you healthy and happy all day.'

The Magic Pass was an unusually straight strip of land that connected the peninsula to the mainland. Legend had it that it was originally an island and when the first settlers came from the mainland and could not cross, they prayed and God answered their prayers by laying a straight but narrow path. Another version was that these early settlers were dissidents from a faraway settlement who were chased by soldiers. When they got to the shore and could not cross, they prayed and God answered their prayers by creating the pass. As soon as they crossed, a high tide came and covered the pass and when the chasing army arrived they thought the dissidents had drowned. The soldiers turned and went back.

By the time Jamil and his grandfather reached what was called Settler's Junction, it was bright enough for the birds to fly around.

Jamil stood and counted the number of birds on a particular tree at the junction. He would normally count till twenty and stop. He shook a low hanging branch to get the birds to fly.

'Peace be with you,' a young man greeted Kamal.

'And with you too,' Kamal replied gently.

'Peace forever,' Jamil chipped in.

Kamal thanked Jamil for greeting a stranger. 'Do you know why we say Peace forever?'

'No.'

'It's because we've never known war.'

It was bright when they arrived at the wooden house in Gariyon. 'Peace to the woman of the house,' Kamal said announcing their arrival.

'Peace to the man returning home,' replied Laila, Jamil's grandmother.

'Men, please,' Kamal said, reminding Laila that Jamil was now a big boy.

'Sorry, men. The little one is not that little anymore.'

'Yes.'

'Did the young man take a dip then?'

'No. His time will come,' Kamal was firm. 'Is everything set for our visitor?'

'Yes,' said Laila and returned to the side of the house where she was squeezing oil out of fish. Jamil knew it was a delicate and time-consuming process.

'The fish does not produce much oil anymore,' she complained. 'Even the size has changed. I cannot understand what they catch these days. It's hard squeezing for oil. Not like when we were younger. Then it was a lot easier.'

'You're right. When the fish gave us our riches,' Kamal said, 'there were fish everywhere. We just walked into the sea with baskets and nets and caught them. Now we have to go very far into the sea to catch these miserable things.'

'Welcome to our beloved peninsula,' greeted Kamal, who was wearing a long rope and perfume and had his arms wide open as Uncle Majid alighted from the boat.

'I'm so happy to see you again,' Majid replied as the two embraced warmly. Uncle Majid leaned on his smooth walking stick fingering his long beard.

'You chose the best time to visit,' Kamal said, still holding his friend.

'I always loved the Season of the Setting Suns,' Uncle Majid admitted, coughing slightly.

'Yes. It's the best time indeed. We're endowed with a lot of sun.'

As close friends they shook hands seven times and embraced again. Jamil liked counting the number of handshakes people made on the peninsula as it signified their relationship: One handshake for total strangers; three for acquaintances; and seven times for really close friends.

'Yes, I can see people still have the trademark smile because of the thirteen hours of sunshine.' He paused. 'What a beautiful place. Honestly I feel better whenever I visit.'

'It's the sun.'

'You are right. It lightens my heart, cures my illness ... even my aching joints,' Majid said with a long laugh.

'Don't exaggerate Majid.'

'I'm not. I definitely feel younger here.' Majid turned to Jamil. 'How's the little one?'

'I'm fine.'

'How old are you now?'

'I'm thirteen years old.'

'How time flies,' Majid said and turned to Kamal. 'You mean it's over ten years since I emigrated?'

'Yes, indeed.'

As they walked back to Gariyon from the port, Jamil carried Majid's bag and wondered why people left their homes to come to the peninsula just for the sun. He had noticed that during the Season of the Setting Suns there were a lot of visitors to the peninsula. This was when churning clouds rolled over slowly from the south and spread widely, creating dramatically coloured skies. During this time, especially late in the afternoons, the skies blazed bright with vivid colours.

As soon as they arrived home, although Jamil was eager to get his present, he was required to wait until he was given the gift. He was not expected to ask. Jamil waited patiently as Majid sat on the veranda facing the setting sun. The old man sat there quietly, just to capture and register the scenery in his memory. After a while, Majid stood up and raised his hands to the sky in prayers. Jamil knew the prayer and joined him: *we are blessed for we are only one step away from heaven!*

Majid told Jamil to go and play. 'I'll see you later. I want to enjoy the sun before it sets.'

Jamil went to the lighthouse where he knew his friend Bashir and the other kids in the neighbourhood would be playing around that time of the day.

'We saw something that resembled the monster,' Bashir said looking scared.

'Really? When? Where?' Jamil asked looking at the sea.

'Just before you came, and there, very far away,' Bashir said, leaning on Jamil to look further into the sea. Bashir was the son of a fisherman and they lived near the lighthouse. Bashir was shorter than Jamil.

'Why do you always see the monster when I'm not here?' Jamil questioned.

'Because the monster does not want you to see it.'

'I want to see the monster.'

'My mother thinks there is nothing like monsters but my father said he saw one when he was a teenager.'

'Maybe monsters show themselves only to teenagers not to adults.'

A triangular formation of white birds flew in from the sea. The boys started singing:

Leke-leke give us rains
Leke-leke give us luck
Leke-leke make us play
Leke-leke show us the sea monster.

By the time Jamil returned home it was getting dark and a parcel was waiting for him on the table. With the permission of the elders, an excited Jamil opened it. It contained a wooden key. Jamil's face changed. He could not understand why Uncle Majid had brought him this present. 'The wooden key was specially carved for you by one of the best carvers in our city. It symbolises success. I hope that it opens all doors for you. Look at it closely, your name is inscribed on it.'

Jamil thanked Uncle Majid.

'Who knows ... he might be the one to bring back the other half of our key,' said Laila. 'I always prayed for the other half to be returned. Life is becoming unbearable here. We need the key to bring back a bit of sanity.'

'That's a dream,' Kamal responded.

'May Jamil be the one that brings the key back,' prayed Laila.

'Any idea where the other half of the golden key is right now?'

'No one knows and no one cares really.'

The next day Jamil showed off his present. 'Uncle Majid says it's a magical key that can open all doors. I hope that one day I'll catch the monster and use this key to lock it up in a shed so that it cannot get out.'

'But you cannot use the key to catch the monster,' Bashir objected.

'I'll use my hands,' said Jamil.

'You must be joking. Monsters are big you know.'

'How big?'

'As big as the lighthouse.'

'Wow. That is three times the size of an ordinary house.'

'Anyway, your key is just a key not a padlock.' Bashir dismissed the idea.

Later in the day, while Jamil was resting, he overheard a conversation between his grandfather and their guest.

'Where were you today?' Kamal asked Majid.

'I went to see an old friend in the House of Samad.'

'How's it there?'

'Not very well I'm afraid,' Majid answered.

'I hardly go there. Things have changed I hear.'

'Yes, very little attention is paid to education these days. When Samad was in charge things were different.'

'Yes, you are right. That was when people used to come from all over the world to study under the leadership of Samad, the scientist and inventor,' Kamal agreed.

The peninsula derived its name from a plant that grew there called Tatasi. No one knew exactly when it was introduced. Some said it was always there, while others argued that sailors brought it from another place. Tatasi was very useful and rich. The leaves could be used for tea, stew, soup and medicines. The flowers were used for perfume and when dried and mixed with other ingredients also made a refreshing and nourishing drink. The root was used for medicines – especially to fight colds, coughs and stomach ache. The seeds were used for spices and soap.

With time an industry grew out of this plant. It was during this time, the Tatasi Boom as it was called, that Kamal came to the peninsula and settled in the Gariyon area where they had a farm. As demand grew so did the methods used to increase supply. Where Tatasi was never planted before, new ways were invented to cultivate it. While it normally took two years from planting and pruning to harvesting – the natural cycle – these new methods meant the cycle was shortened to one year. Special sheds were built to produce Tatasi all year round. New species were engineered that could be mass produced in six months. The average height of a Tatasi plant was that of a human being but the new species were three times the size.

The two old men talked about the plant that had meant a lot over their long lives.

'Those were the hard times. We really worked hard on the farms.'

'They were also challenging and the wealth was equally distributed which led to our unity and we were all happy.'

'The plant is leading to our unhappiness and will ultimately lead to our destruction,' Kamal added gloomily.

'Hmm,' Majid thought for a while fingering his grey beard. 'I'm really worried for the peninsula. I see some things that really trouble me. These are small things that are new. For example, what has surprised me most is the way people seem to talk less to each other. When they do, it's all about money. I've heard some phrases that are new here. How much am I going to make? What's my cut? What's in there for me? I was told in the House of Samad that people have stopped learning for learning's sake.'

'This is all down to Tatasi,' Kamal took up the conversation. 'We are so dependent on this plant that we do not see the negative things it's doing to our lives. What was once considered a sin is now normal practice. Remember we never knew anything like hoarding. We shared or took what satisfied our needs.'

'That's right,' Majid concurred.

'Now people build bigger houses to hide things.' Kamal paused and drank the Tatasi nourishing drink and chewed dried fish. 'What should have been a blessing is now a curse. A healthy plant is making the people sick.'

'What happened to the policy of "a drop of honey for everyone?"' Majid asked.

'It was scrapped ages ago. We are all after profit from Tatasi and the new king simply does not think the proceeds from Tatasi should be distributed among the people.'

'What's he doing with all the money?'

'He's building a huge palace on the hills in Baritaye.'

'What a funny old world.'

CHAPTER FOUR

The Twin Tragedy

Jamil had a dream about the wooden key. He dreamt that the key had somehow pulled him off the ground and enabled him to fly. In the next scene the key allowed Jamil to swim with ease underwater. The key also enabled Jamil to glide. All this took place somewhere outside the peninsula, and with many children watching. People gathered to see Jamil perform with his magic key. The last scene involved Jamil rolling around on the beach with the key in his hands yet without a single grain of sand on his body. When he awoke, he remembered vividly that the dream ended with the key disappearing. He did not know where it had gone and in the morning could not say whether he actually found it or not. To his relief, the wooden key presented to him by Uncle Majid was at his bedside. The loss of the dream key affected him all day. Although he was in possession of the real wooden key, the loss of the one in the dream meant something he could not explain.

In the evening when the two old men settled down on the veranda for their chat, Jamil asked them about the golden key of the peninsula. He had heard several stories about it and it was because of the mysteries surrounding it that Jamil volunteered to be a member of the Guardians of the Key Brigade.

His grandfather, Kamal, was the first to speak. 'Long before Majid and I settled here, the people went through a very bad period of drought, famine, disease and flooding. This was preceded by a powerful earthquake. They chose a particular day to reflect and ask for forgiveness as it was understood that their bad behaviour had brought about these misfortunes. One year later, they noticed that things changed for better. They began to prosper again. Then they decided to dedicate a day for thanksgiving. They called it Day of Renewal. Some extraordinary things happened that day. First, the sun was partially covered for a long time. In the evening they noticed that there were mysterious lights every-where. The people panicked. As they ran from one part of the peninsula to the other, lightning struck in two different places. These two places remained illuminated for a while. Curious inhabitants went to find out what the source of light was. To their astonishment, they saw two halves of a golden key in both illuminated places.

'These Gifts from the Heavens,' Kamal continued, 'were then fixed together and guarded. In time the key came to symbolise peace, prosperity, unity, stability and balance. As you must have noticed, every year the people line the streets on the Day of Renewal to touch the key and pray for protection and blessings. Just before you were born, something extraordinary happened during the Day of Renewal. The people were ordered not to touch the key and some people reported that the one that was carried did not look like the old one. A year later, the people noticed that the new key was in a box, which meant that the people could not touch it. Since then, many things have been going wrong in this land. It's been one disaster after another. The absence of the old key affects our lives, especially on the Day of Renewal.'

'Yes, grandpa,' Jamil joined in 'last year my mouth just wouldn't open when I wanted to sing praises. My friend Bashir had a very strange experience. He was able to sing praises only from the last line to the first. He and I could not perform simple acrobatic displays. It was as if our feet were fixed to the ground. It was very scary.'

'I was confused,' Kamal continued. 'All day I had foggy thoughts which I put down to old age. I drank lots of Tatasi nourishing drink but was still confused all day. We were still in a state of shock when the sun set and instead of the usual dances and mass celebrations, for no known reason, the people spent the evening in silence. Something was missing but no one knew what it was. Just when we were about to go to bed, suddenly and without any warning, a curtain of light danced across the skies. I didn't see it at first. I was weak and resting. A lot of people were frightened.'

'Yes,' Jamil confirmed, 'I was excited but some people fainted while others screamed with fear.'

Kamal continued, 'When I came out I noticed the lights and saw that they became brighter and brighter and the displays became more vivid and wild. There were lights of many colours dancing in the skies at the same time.

'From here,' Kamal said, moving to a particular spot on the veranda, 'I could see ghostly illuminations everywhere. They then disappeared as the whole peninsula brightened up. It was as if a huge lamp had been lit, wasn't it Jamil?'

'Yes, I remember the first red lights that flowed in the sky like a river over there and then disappeared. Then new lights came. Then they all disappeared. Then all the lights came on at once. It became so bright that we walked down the streets singing and dancing. Suddenly the night turned to day.'

'What was the cause?' Majid asked with concern.

'No one knows but it was really scary,' said Kamal. 'I'll never forget that night: the night the skies caught fire!'

'Has it got anything to do with the key?'

'Maybe. Some people believe the half-key that was in the peninsula disappeared and that was why the skies that gave us the key were angry. Some said the lights were signs of good things to come. To me personally, they were signs of terror that would befall the peninsula.'

'Is it possible to bring the other half of the key back to the peninsula?' Jamil asked when Kamal paused.

'Yes it is possible if you know where it is. Unfortunately we don't know where it is at the moment. I had always dreamt of going on an adventure and somehow bringing the key back. I'm too old for such dreams now.'

'Not even Tatasi drink will roll back the years,' Majid joked and turned to Jamil. 'It is indeed possible to bring it back. In life many things are possible.'

'Do you think I could bring it back?'

'What an interesting question!' said Majid. 'As you have shown a capacity to think on your feet, I think it is possible.' Majid paused and placed his hand on Jamil's shoulder, 'If you dream of doing something and you put that dream into action, and if this is done honestly and sincerely on your chosen path, then fate will make what seems impossible possible.'

'In other words, if you seek, you will get,' Kamal concluded.

The month-long festivities to celebrate the opening of the new palace had drained Jamil's energy. He was looking forward to the last day when he would be one of those who would carry the key in the box to the doors of the new palace. Jamil was excited. He and others had practised their movements so many times that he boasted, 'I can perform my role with my eyes closed.'

The day before the official opening of the palace, Kamal had warned Jamil in veiled language: 'Beware of the curse from the sky.'

'What do you mean?'

'Have you looked at the sky today?'

'No, what's up there?'

'People are so busy enjoying themselves that they pay no attention to the important things in life. There have been warning signs in the sky over the peninsula but very few people have noticed it.'

Jamil did not pay attention to his grandfather. He was too engrossed in the festivities. When he eventually did look up at the sky he noticed some unusual cloud formations, and it occurred to him that there were normally no clouds in the dry season. But he simply shrugged and continued with the celebrations.

The Guardians of the Key Brigade carried the golden box in a group of four. They marched slowly with it for about two hundred metres then handed it over to another group. Jamil's group was the last. His heartbeat increased as the golden box approached. Without any mistakes, the handover was made as rehearsed many times. They marched slowly, Jamil in front, towards the imposing palace. The public clapped and sang praises.

Jamil felt proud and smiled as they marched. Despite the loud noise around him, he could hear Kamal's voice in his head: 'This is not the real key. It's fake and will not save the peninsula.' But Kamal's voice was not strong enough to suppress his enthusiasm and sense of duty. Jamil marched on with pride and satisfaction.

Jamil and others carried the golden box that contained the key up the stairs to the massive doors of the palace. The king, the queen, the princes and princesses and other dignitaries rose to their feet as the box approached. At the designated spot, the group stopped as commanded by Jamil. They handed the box to two guards who opened it and gave the key to the king. After a short speech in which he promised better times ahead for the people of Tatasi Peninsula, the king opened the doors majestically. There was a huge ovation.

'I'm so happy everything went well,' Bashir said.

'Yes, I'm so excited. I was so close to the king and did you see the way the Queen looked at us? I saw the key at close range also. I'm so happy.'

'I'm so tired. Let's go.'

The two boys headed towards Gariyon. There were fireworks all over the peninsula. After about half-an-hour, it began to rain. Jamil looked at Bashir. They were stunned.

'What's going on?' Bashir asked Jamil.

'I don't know.'

'Maybe it's part of the celebrations.'

'I doubt it.'

They were beginning to feel scared. There was definitely some-thing unusual in the air. 'Something extraordinary is happening,' someone shouted to confirm their fears. 'This is not normal,' another voice screamed.

As they ran towards Gariyon, the sky was illuminated from afar by a fork of lightning that was followed by a loud crack of thunder. Jamil was excited and frightened at the same time. 'This is scary,' he said to himself. The two boys could not make sense of what was going on. The lightning was spectacular. As they stood perplexed, they saw three different types of lightning; one that stayed, hanging, in the sky; one that struck from the cloud to the ground; and a third that struck upwards from the ground to the clouds.

'Look at that. It goes from the ground up,' Jamil said.

Jamil and Bashir were not sure if it was part of the ceremonies. They ignored some boys chanting 'Long Live the King! Long Live the Key!'

In the meantime there was more and more lightning and it was striking closer and closer. 'Wow!' screamed Jamil, when an enormous bolt struck from cloud to earth. The closer the lightning came the more frightened they were. The two boys were no longer enjoying the spectacle. People began to scream and run around helplessly as they felt electric discharges from the lightning.

'Something is biting me all over my body,' Bashir screamed in the darkness. Jamil began again to run towards Gariyon but when a powerful clap of thunder shook the entire area, he stopped. He was shocked and dazed. All around him the thunderstorm raged. Then it stopped abruptly. The sudden silence confused everybody. Jamil worried about everything and everybody, especially his parents who were in the Baritaye area and his grandparents in the Gariyon area of the peninsula.

Jamil thought he felt the ground shake but was not sure. Then it happened again and again. There were eruptions somewhere but he could not say what exactly was happening. He could see the flare of fires far out to sea and was relieved they were not closer. Jamil convinced himself it was a volcanic eruption far out in the sea. He stood on the spot not knowing what to do. The eruptions continued for some time.

Gradually thick smoke covered the peninsula. Jamil started to cough. He ran into the nearest house and closed the windows. Just when he thought he was safe a powerful earthquake struck the peninsula. The house shook. The walls cracked and parts of the ceiling collapsed. Jamil ran out of the house screaming and frightened. So many houses were crashing down around him. He watched as people ran around aimlessly screaming and wailing.

There were cries from near and far. Cries and shouts everywhere. Jamil was paralysed by fear. In the darkness, Jamil could only sit with his eyes closed to all around him. It was too much. He knew he ought to stand up, be grateful he was alive, and run to either Gariyon or Baritaye to help people – those not as fortunate as himself – but he could not. He began to cry in the darkness.

When what appeared to be the sun rose over the debris and destruction, a dazed Jamil opened his eyes to the reality around him. From the highest point of Babulosa, he could see that most houses were in ruins. The scale of the calamity shocked him. After the earthquake, houses had caught fire. Some were still burning. There were floods in other parts too. It was as if a giant had walked through the peninsula, kicking and smashing houses and occasionally setting some ablaze as it walked along. Streets and neighbourhoods were piles of rubble except for a few houses, mainly old wooden dwellings.

He walked amid the debris and destruction to what used to be Baritaye. Half of the area including the new palace had crumbled into the sea. Jamil sat down by the edge of the cliff from where he could see parts of the destroyed palace lying in the sea. He wailed when it dawned on him that it would take a miracle for his parents to have survived. They'd been working in the palace that evening.

He mustered all the energy left in his body to walk to Gariyon. It took Jamil a long time to find his way to the other side of the peninsula where his grandparents lived. From afar he could see that the house was not destroyed but he was too dazed to believe it.

As he approached, he smiled for the first time when he saw his grandparents in front of the house. He ran and hugged them in tears.

'Your parents are safe and well. They were here some moments ago but went out looking for you,' Kamal said hugging Jamil.

'You must have missed each other on the way,' said Laila holding him firmly.

'There is so much destruction and death everywhere,' Jamil said.

'Well, young man, we cannot say we were not warned,' said Kamal.

'Enough,' the grandmother shouted. 'This is not the time for such talk.'

'I'm going to look for my parents.'

'Come and see,' the grandmother said. 'Come and see, little one, the work of nature.' Pointing at what used to be the Magic Pass, she said. 'See the pass is gone, destroyed by the earthquake.

'Nothing links us to the mainland?' a curious Jamil asked.

'Nothing. We're on an island now,' she replied raising her hands up.

'That's exciting,' Jamil thought.

'Also see, the new island is elevated there and moved closer to the mainland.'

'Amazing! Tatasi Island,' said Jamil.

'Yes, young man. A new island and it is called The Cursed Island,' Kamal said with a dry smile.

Jamil decided to go and look for his parents. As he walked he saw destruction all over the new island. People were frantically trying to rescue others, while some just sat, dazed by the scale of death and destruction around them. He heard the faint sound of a goat bleating in a collapsed building. Jamil began to search frantically. He kept on digging until he got to where the goat was. Jamil pulled the small goat out successfully. It was dazed and injured and could hardly walk. Jamil carried it to his grandparents' house.

'That's very good of you. Anything that can be saved should be saved,' said Laila.

'You and I are lucky,' Jamil said to the goat later, while feeding it. 'We survived. Did you see the destruction around? So many people perished but we are lucky, we survived, we are the lucky ones. That's an idea. From now on I'll call you Lucky.'

Later Bashir found him. 'I'm so happy to see you,' said Bashir.

'What happened to you here?' Jamil asked pointing at his elbow.

'Part of the house fell on me but I was so lucky.'

'We all are. I have even named the goat Lucky.'

'Have you seen what happened to the palace?' asked Bashir.

'Yes and have you seen what happened to the pass?'

'Yes. Have you heard about the monsters?'

'You know I don't believe in monsters,' replied Jamil.

'Haven't you heard the cry of the real monster?' Bashir asked.

'No I haven't,' Jamil answered.

'Have you seen the monster's smoke?'

'What are you talking about?' a puzzled Jamil asked.

'I've heard strange noises from the sea and have seen smoke rise from the sea too.'

'Smoke from the sea?'

'Yes, Jamil. There are noises and smoke from the sea. The smoke has a very strong smell and makes people dizzy.'

There was something in Bashir's eyes and voice that made Jamil believe the story of the monster. 'You mean there are monsters around us?' Jamil asked.

'Yes, there are monsters around the island,' Bashir replied glancing around them nervously. 'Believe me Jamil, I saw a boat full of people tossed into the air and that was it.'

'What do you mean? What happened?'

'First there was a monster's cry, then there was thick smoke that covered the boat and then the boat was tossed into the air and that was it,' Bashir explained, still nervous. 'When the smoke cleared I didn't see anyone swim back to the island...I didn't see anyone,' he emphasized.

'What happened to them?'

'They all disappeared.'

'Maybe they'll come back one day. Maybe they swam across somehow,' Jamil said trying to be optimistic.

'No Jamil, once the smoke cleared, there was nothing, no one at all,' Bashir explained.

Jamil's heart began to pound heavily. Suddenly he thought he heard strange noises in the distance. He looked round nervously. From the corner of his eyes Jamil thought he saw a strange figure gliding towards them. 'Monster!' he screamed.

'Where?'

'There…' Jamil pointed into the distance.

'But there's nothing there,' Bashir said looking around nervously.

'I thought I saw something moving towards us,' Jamil's voice was shaking. 'I'm scared.'

'Everyone is scared on the island.'

Moments later there was a loud noise from the sea. It was a mixture of deep grunts and shrieks. It pierced through the skies of the island.

'That's the monster's cry,' screamed Bashir and began to run.

Jamil ran as fast as he could toward his grandparents' house.

Jamil's mother screamed with joy as he ran into the house. 'Thank God you're alive,' she said and embraced him. 'We've been very worried and your father is out there looking for you.'

'I heard the monster's cry,' Jamil said still panting.

'Did you see it?' Laila asked.

'No I didn't. As soon as I heard the cry I began to run.'

'This is very scary,' Jamil's mother said still holding her son. 'Life on the new island will be terrible. We're all scared of what will happen next.'

'We're all prisoners of the monster now,' Kamal pointed out.

Jamil's father entered the room panting. 'The monster just passed,' he said.

'Did you see it?' Jamil asked.

'No I didn't. I don't think anyone has seen it yet. It hides behind the thick smoke it releases.'

'My friend said there are several monsters,' said Jamil.

'No one knows exactly whether there's one or several monsters out there,' Jamil's father added.

'There's definitely something out there,' said Laila casting her worried look at Jamil. 'I saw thick smoke and heard strange noises but didn't think it'll be a monster. Too many terrible things are happening to us.'

There was silence for a couple of minutes.

'Who knows what tomorrow will bring,' started Kamal with a sense of resignation to no one in particular. 'The earthquake was bad enough with all the destructions around. Now we have a monster or several monsters around us.'

There was another spell of silence.

'This is a catastrophe that has befallen us,' Jamil's father broke the silence. 'I was told that the volcanic eruption has made the sea waters around us so hot that no one can swim across and those who choose to cross by boats are devoured by the monsters.'

'Yes,' Kamal added his voice. 'The waters are so hot that the fish are either dead or gone.'

Jamil's father asked: 'Has anyone noticed that the smoke from the volcanic eruption is hanging over us? I've noticed that it's not moving.'

'Oh my God!' exclaimed Kamal who was despondent. 'The worst things that could happen to us are happening right now. If the smoke remains hanging over the island, it would be worse than the earthquake or the monster. The smoke will affect everything—from the air we breathe to the food we eat. The smoke will choke us to death, it will prevent the sun from shining on us and will stop rain from falling. All plants especially Tatasi cannot grow under such conditions. Everything will be affected by this cloud which I'll call the Devil's Carpet,' Kamal paused. He looked at Jamil and continued.' This twin tragedy will finish us all slowly. I fear for the future of this island, if we have any at all.'

CHAPTER FIVE

The Dream

One day, about six months after the Twin Tragedy, Jamil walked with his pet goat Lucky to where the children of Gariyon area usually met. From afar, he could see Bashir and about a dozen other children marching and singing.

'*Monster Monster you'll die*
Monster Monster you'll die'

Jamil joined the parade that usually culminated in a vow to kill the monster. After the initial parade, Jamil was given a catapult. 'When the time comes, I'll tell you how we're going to kill the monster,' Bashir said and advised him to start gathering stones. Jamil knew Bashir had a plan to attack the monster at a particular place and time. Bashir, who was the Commander of the Tatasi Brigade Against the Monster, kept his plans secret.

Jamil sat under a tree with his pet by his side. 'Lucky, you see, we're planning to kill the monster. I don't know how because it's a secret. The monster must not know how we intend to kill it. We have to kill the monster before it kills us all. Look there Lucky, the volcano has stopped erupting and now we have a new island. My main dream is to kill the monster and then go to wherever the other half of the key is and bring it back to the island so that we can have stability again. My secret wish is for us to be the first to step on the new island. I want us to make history. Some people say the monster lives there – that's why nobody has ever been there. Immediately we kill the monster, you and I will go straight to the new island. Maybe it'll be called Lucky Island. After that you and I will leave the island and go out in search of the golden key,' he confided in his pet.

Jamil closed his eyes and dozed off.

In his sleep he had a dream. One afternoon Jamil and Bashir were walking down a narrow path with tall trees.

'Look at that big river over there,' Bashir said starting a conversation.

'Look at the mountain there. I want to climb to the top,' Jamil said.

'Why?' asked Bashir.

'I heard that whoever climbs the mountain will have their dreams come true.'

'All right, let's go then,' Bashir said pushing forward.

'But how are we going to cross the river?' wondered Jamil.

'You're right. No boats, no bridges. Nothing. Let's go.'

'Let's keep walking. There might just be a way out,' Jamil urged.

'Hey, look at that,' exclaimed Bashir.

'What?'

'A crocodile coming out of the river,' Bashir shouted.

The two boys started to run away. An invisible force stopped them and a voice from nowhere said: 'This crocodile will not harm you. This crocodile will help you.'

The boys stopped and bravely walked towards the crocodile. 'How can I help you boys?' asked the crocodile.

'We want to cross the river,' Bashir answered.

'Where are you going to?' the crocodile asked further.

'We want to climb the mountain over there,' Jamil answered.

'There are actually five mountains. This is the first one and getting to the top of this is one of the most difficult challenges in the world, but the reward for getting to *The Roof of The World* is that you'll get to see what is called The Smile of the Creator. Whoever sees the smile of the creator will have at least three wishes fulfilled. So boys, while you're up there and if lucky enough to see the smile, make a wish immediately … You'll know it when you see it.'

'Wow! How do we get there?' Jamil asked.

'There are many paths. You'll have to choose the path that suits you.'

'How many paths?' asked Bashir. 'How do we know the path that is right?'

'So many paths. The best path will take you down first before you go up.'

'But that's difficult,' said Bashir.

'You think getting to the summit of the mountain is easy?' posed the crocodile.

'What are the dangers?' Jamil asked.

'There are three dangerous animals on the mountain. The python, the lion and the gorilla. You cannot avoid them.' The crocodile taught them the tricks of getting round the dangerous animals.

'How do we know if we are on the right path?'

'Good question. If halfway through your ascent you go through what is called The Prayer House in the Stone then you're on the right path.'

'How do we know when we get there?' Jamil probed further.

'You'll know. You'll be on your knees.'

'How do you know all these things?' Bashir asked. 'Have you ever been up there?'

'No I haven't. The luck of a crocodile is not on the mountains.'

'How do we cross the river?' Jamil asked, eager to climb the mountain.

'That's the easiest part of it. Jump on my back and I'll take you across,' the crocodile said and crawled to the river. The boys sat on the crocodile and it carried them across the wide river.

'I think this is the best way,' Bashir said pointing at a path. 'It goes straight and we can start climbing.'

'But the crocodile said we have to go down to find the best way up,' argued Jamil.

The two boys continued to argue. Bashir's suggestion led to a dead-end. Jamil decided to take the lead. As they climbed they discovered that there were many paths. They were initially confused, but they continued walking. Soon they reached another dead-end. There was a cliff to the left and a cave right in front of them.

'Oh my God!' Bashir screamed.

'What is it?' Jamil asked, frightened.

'There are bones in the cave. We're in front of the lion's den.' They turned and ran for their lives.

'The lion must be somewhere. I'm scared,' said Bashir.

'Let's not think about the animals … just how to get to the top,' Jamil urged.

They took another path. When they were tired, they decided to rest under a tree. The boys dozed off. Jamil woke to see a lion about twenty metres away walking majestically through the high grasses. He nudged Bashir awake beside him. The lion was looking at them and licking its mouth. Bashir panicked. He wanted to run but Jamil grabbed him and pulled him back. 'Stand still and be brave or you'll die young.' The lion moved slowly towards them. They both stood firm on their feet. 'Just follow my orders okay?' Jamil said to Bashir. 'Rule number one: No Fear! Rule number two: Don't run. The lion can run faster than you and it's probably hungry.'

Jamil stood firm and fixed his eyes on the approaching big cat. He took two steps forward. 'We're not afraid of you,' Jamil started talking to the advancing lion. 'We'll look straight into your eyes. You may be the king of the jungle but we are not afraid of you. Come … keep coming … yes … keep coming … we'll not run … you want one of us to run so that you can chase and catch … no way … we'll not be the hunted, okay?'

The lion stopped for a moment and looked straight at the boys. Suddenly it charged forward hoping that one of the boys would panic and run. The boys stood firm. Jamil looked straight into its eyes without blinking and the lion stopped. After five minutes of the tense stand off, the lion wagged its tail and disappeared into the bushes.

'I was really scared,' Bashir said shaking.

'I was too but you have to be brave to get to the top.'

As they continued their ascent, they heard a strange sort of hissing noise. It was as if someone or something was whistling at them. Jamil hoped it was a human being coming down from the top who could give them advice on how best to get up there. He looked up hoping to see someone. As they continued their ascent, they heard the noise again. They were now convinced the noise was behind them. They became alert and anxious.

'I think it's the gorilla hiding somewhere,' Bashir suggested.

'But we should have seen it. It's too big to hide in the trees.'

'You never know with these animals.'

The two boys continued walking. 'The last thing I want to meet now is a mountain gorilla,' Bashir said, looking round nervously. There was a carpet of dry, crunchy leaves. There were no telltale signs of any animals.

They heard the noise again. This time they stopped and decided to survey the surroundings. Suddenly Bashir screamed.

'What is it?'

'It's the python,' he whispered, pointing to a snake a few feet away from them.

'Remember the instructions of the crocodile?'

'Yes.'

The two boys stood like statues. They placed their right feet on their left knees and stretched their hands wide. This was to create the impression that they were fixed objects and not living, moving beings that could be attacked and eaten.

'Hey young men,' the python said, getting closer to them. 'I know the trick already. Relax. Put your feet and hands down. I've been following you. I'm not going to harm you. I can see you're lost. You're taking the wrong path to the summit. Follow me and I'll show you the right path.' The python was now very close to them. Jamil remembered that the crocodile had specifically mentioned the python was a dangerous animal. He hesitated. 'Thanks, python, our instincts tell us we are indeed on the right path.'

'We know where we are going,' Bashir emphasised.

'This has been my home since I was born and I know all the paths. I've helped so many people get to the top,' the python explained.

'How can you help us then?' Bashir asked.

'I can take the two of you to the top in record time. I'll make sure we avoid the most dangerous path on earth. It's called the Path of No Return. One wrong step and that's it. I know how to take you round it. I also know the best way to make you avoid The Prayer House in the Stone.'

'Why? The crocodile thinks it's exciting!' exclaimed Jamil.

'The crocodile has never been beyond the river, do not believe anything he told you. I've been here. This is my home and I know every nook and corner. This place called The Prayer House in the Stone humiliates people. You'll bend and crawl on your knees through dark tunnels. Do you really want to bend down and crawl? It's very scary and I will make sure I take you round it.'

Jamil did not trust the snake and politely declined.

'This is dangerous and I'm terrified,' Bashir said as he steadied himself to avoid slipping down a dangerous gorge. Stones were rolling down the edge of the mountain. Jamil turned round just in time to grab him and save him from falling with them. Jamil pulled him up and they resumed their ascent.

'We should have accepted the offer from the snake,' Bashir said as they took one dangerous step after another. Jamil did not answer. He had only one thing in mind: how to pass the Path of No Return without falling into the deep gorges below.

'Don't look left or right, okay?' Jamil shouted as he led Bashir along the treacherous path. As soon as they passed the stretch of narrow slippery path, the two boys found themselves in the mouth of a tunnel just wide enough to take one person at a time. For the first time Jamil was genuinely afraid. He decided not to show it but to brave it out.

'What if the gorilla is waiting for us in there?' Bashir asked.

'We have to fight. We have no alternative now do we?'

'I'm terribly scared,' Bashir confessed.

'What if there's nothing?' Jamil said and took the first step into the tunnel. Ten steps in he asked, 'Are you following me?'

'Yes,' Bashir whispered.

After about twenty metres, it began to get brighter. Jamil could not say where the lights were coming from but it appeared to him that the stones deep in the tunnel were emitting light. As he walked slowly, he heard the faint sound of water flowing.

'Is that water or am I imagining things?' Jamil asked.

'I thought I heard something like that too,' Bashir answered.

They walked slowly on, moving closer and closer to the sound. Eventually they turned a corner and there, before them, was the source: it was a waterfall deep in the mountain. There was a sort of magic to the whole environment; the waterfall was brightened by light from the stones.

'I think we've reached a dead-end. I cannot see a way out of this place,' Bashir said looking around. 'It's all rocks around here.'

'The crocodile would have told us,' Jamil said starting to touch the bright rocks on either side of the tunnel. 'There must be a way out. I don't want to believe it's a dead end. We just can't go back now.' Jamil touched and pushed the rocks as he probed for a way through. Unexpectedly, one of the rocks he pushed moved and suddenly he found another tunnel, smaller but well lit. He went on his knees and started to crawl with Bashir following.

'Do you know where we're going?' Bashir asked.

'I don't know but we're not lost,' Jamil responded.

After about ten minutes of crawling, they reached the exit. They emerged happy, relieved and dazed. They had no time to talk about their experiences. The vegetation had changed. The trees were shorter and well spaced. There was light and the air was fresher. The tired boys decided to rest under one of the trees. One after the other they closed their eyes and slept.

Hours later when Jamil opened his eyes, they were met by two filmy, brownish penetrating eyes looking at him from a very close range. The mountain gorilla appeared very relaxed as it sat on a rock with a branch of a tree in its left hand. Jamil tried to avoid eye contact. He was genuinely frightened. He looked down enough to be able to see the lower part of the gorilla. From time to time, he would steal glances at it. Jamil made up his mind not to run. He was too tired and weak anyway and the gorilla knew the terrain very well. Jamil tapped Bashir gently who screamed the moment he opened his eyes. The two stood up looking down, trying to avoid any eye contact.

'Welcome to my territory,' the gorilla said after a prolonged silence. 'Are you going up or coming down?'

'Going up,' Jamil replied as calmly as possible.

'You've a long way to go but I can take the two of you there. The two of you can sit on my back but that would be a bit difficult. You may not know this, a gorilla can walk on two legs. I'll carry both of you with my arms. Or I could carry both of you on my broad shoulders. As you can see they are really broad. One on each side will not be a burden at all for me.' The gorilla stood up to show its shoulders. 'I'll take both of you right to the top. You'll be safe from other animals and have a good view of the mountain.'

'I don't trust the gorilla and its body odour stinks,' Bashir whispered.

Still avoiding eye contact, Jamil said to the gorilla. 'We're very grateful. We've come this far on our own and enjoyed it and we'd like to get to the top by ourselves.'

The gorilla was visibly angry. Beating its chest and stamping its right leg, the beast shouted. 'I'm the boss here. This is my territory and nobody rejects my offers here. This is disobedience. You think I'm going to harm you? I'm here to help you.'

'Let's accept it and go. I'm afraid of what it'll do and honestly I'm tired,' said Bashir.

'No way,' countered Jamil.

'Shut up,' the gorilla shouted at Jamil angrily. 'You don't know what you are talking about and you don't know where you are going anyway.'

'We're on a journey,' Jamil stated firmly.

'Shut up.'

'Leave us alone,' Jamil stood his ground and looked straight into the eyes of the gorilla.

'Nobody refuses my offers here.'

Jamil and the gorilla stared at each other for a while. The gorilla looked shocked. 'Get lost! Go away!' It shouted several times, stamping its feet on the ground and repeatedly thumping its chest.

'Get lost too. Go away. Leave us alone,' Jamil shouted back beating his chest.

The mountain gorilla grabbed the nearest tree and shook it violently in anger. It screamed several times and walked away into the bushes.

The boys were elated.

'I couldn't stand its body odour,' Jamil said laughing. 'Let's rest and do the final ascent at dawn as suggested by the crocodile.'

'I'm tired too.'

The two boys found somewhere to sit and looked at each other in disbelief. 'At last, we are just a few hundred metres away from our goal,' Jamil said with a big smile on his face.

'What we initially thought was impossible,' Bashir confessed.

The next morning, the early sunrays filtered through the clouds onto the faces of the boys.

'I've got a headache,' complained Bashir.

'It's because we're far from the ground,' Jamil explained. 'Once we get to the top, you'll be fine.'

'Can't wait to see what the crocodile said was the Smile of the Creator,' Bashir added.

With renewed energy, they started the last part of the ascent. They did not even stop to look back at the view, before hurrying into the clouds. As they entered the clouds, Jamil felt as if something was pulling him from the front and something was pushing him from behind. He felt a great sense of ease.

Jamil was the first to emerge. When he saw what was before them, he was overwhelmed by the magnificent sight and his great sense of accomplishment. Sensing Bashir behind him still in the clouds, he turned back, grabbed him and told him to close his eyes. After guiding him forwards a few steps he said, 'You can now open them.'

Bashir was ecstatic. The two boys ran into the space above the clouds and fell on their knees and cried. Jamil could not believe his eyes. The vast space, the clouds that appeared as a carpet, the sun, wow!

Jamil climbed further taking in the captivating view and fresh air that soothed his lungs. There was no sign saying WELCOME TO THE ROOF OF THE WORLD but it was clear this was it.

Almost everything here was magical. Jamil looked round and could not help thinking that almost anything was possible here. From where he stood, Jamil could see the other four mountains. 'The crocodile was right. See, there are four other mountains there,' Jamil said.

'And that's the lake there,' Bashir said with equal excitement.

They walked to the lake. Jamil went to the highest point on the edge of the lake and climbed it. 'I'm on top of the world,' he shouted several times. He looked closely at the lake again. As he was about to climb down, he noticed something unusual, something that touched him all over his body. Seen from that angle the water did in fact mirror the sky which seemed like – just as the crocodile had said – a smile. Jamil made two wishes while looking at the smile: to kill the monster, and to bring back the key. As soon as he finished, the smile disappeared. Jamil was happy to have had the experience. 'Yes, this place does exist. I can see it. I can feel it and I made my wishes.'

As the boys continued to survey the lake, they noticed a spring at the edge that produced fresh water. They drank from it and rested. It was not too hot. Hours later Jamil looked for the deep end of the lake and dived into it. The two boys swam until they were satisfied.

'When are we going down?' Bashir asked

'Let's go down tomorrow,' suggested Jamil. 'I want us to experience sunset here. Imagine what it would be like at midnight with all the stars!'

'We've a lot to tell the crocodile when we return.'

Jamil felt dizzy and tried to balance himself. 'Is it me or is it the mountain?

'What do you mean?' Bashir asked.

'Something is moving … I can feel something move.'

'I'm fine. I feel nothing,' Bashir said.

'Look,' Jamil screamed. 'My legs are off the ground.'

'What's going on?'

'I'm about to fly.'

Jamil enjoyed the strange sensation of taking off. He took

control and began to glide in the wide horizon over the mountain. When he went round the summit of the first mountain, he glided over the second and began to hear echoes of his name from the valleys and gorges below. Then he glided over the third and fourth mountain experiencing the same strange sound of his name echoing in the valleys and gorges below. He could not understand how the people recognised him from such a distance and knew his name. Who were they? What did they look like? Why his name? What did they want?

While gliding over the last mountain, where the echoes of his name were strongest, he could hear them shouting 'JAMIL, JAMIL, JAMIL.' He decided the best thing to do was to touch down and meet these people. He glided down slowly and as soon as his feet touched the ground he woke up from his sleep.

Jamil opened his eyes slowly. Lucky was standing and staring at him, eager to leave. Jamil rubbed his eyes several times when he realised he was still on the island and it had all been a dream. Jamil could hear the other children marching and singing under the command of Bashir:

Monster Monster you'll die
Monster Monster you'll die
Very soon, you'll die
Monster Monster you'll die
Very soon we'll kill you
Monster Monster you'll die

Jamil and Lucky joined the parade.

CHAPTER SIX

Jamil Engages the Monster

The people of Tatasi Island continued to live in fear of the monster. No one gave a definitive picture of what it really looked like. It appeared in different forms to different people. Some called it a monster with a thousand mouths because it was believed it could devour any living thing on the island at any time. It was called the monster with a thousand stomachs because it was believed it could eat as many living things as possible without being satisfied. Some people called it the monster with a thousand hands because it was believed it could grab anything it wanted – in the sea, on land and in the air.

There was a general belief that the monster would eventually kill and eat all living things on the island – only then would it perish. There was however a general belief that should someone successfully swim across to the mainland the power of the monster would be broken and it would die. Several people had attempted swimming across but failed. Either they drowned or they were devoured by the monster.

More recently, the people had started to believe that in order to punish them further, the monster had released smaller evil monsters: little vampires that attacked people at night. These mini-monsters were smaller than bats but look like monkeys with pointed mouths that were designed to suck the blood of the people. It was believed that before they sucked the blood, these mini-monsters released some kind of anaesthetic saliva that numbed the area they chose to suck from and this enabled them to suck the victims without any pain. The mini-monsters had never been seen during daylight and no one had ever seen their sanctuary.

With time the people noticed a pattern in the movement of the monster. They knew when it was active and these periods were called Monster Curfew Hours. This was the time it was most likely to attack. Then there were Monster Free Hours when the people thought it was least likely to attack them.

'It's all clear,' Kamal told Jamil one afternoon. 'You can go out and about now. The monster is at rest but please be vigilant.'

'Yes, please remember, a monster remains a monster,' Laila added. 'Are you taking Lucky with you?'

'Yes.'

'Be careful. Should you notice anything unusual, please take cover somewhere,' advised Laila.

'Will do,' Jamil said and stopped on his way out. 'Grandpa, it's almost a year since the monster appeared. Do you know how long it's going to live?'

'No one knows.'

'Is it possible for someone to kill it?'

'With what?'

'One thousand stones from catapults for example.'

'I doubt it but in life everything is possible,' Kamal paused. 'Killing the monster is a possibility but the person must get everything right.'

At the lighthouse Jamil told Bashir, 'Honestly, I don't think we can kill the monster with one thousand stones.'

'Why do you think so?'

'What if it disappears into the sea the moment we start throwing the stones? What if the monster releases so much smoke that we cannot see it? What if the monster makes so much noise that we cannot throw the stones? The monster needs a bait to keep it in focus in order to be the target.'

'What did your grandpa say about killing the monster?'

'He said it is possible but we have to be patient. Everything has its time and when the time comes the monster will die.'

'Well he can wait. We can't. We have to kill the monster. We want to liberate our island. Once we kill the monster we shall all be free ...' Bashir suddenly stopped and hid behind a wall. They heard the familiar grunts and groans of the monster nearby. Jamil looked out but saw nothing unusual.

'My grandpa said the monster is becoming very desperate

now and that means trouble for all of us. He said many things are changing and these changes are affecting the monster.'

'Like what?' Bashir asked still hiding.

'For example, the monster liked it when the Devil's Carpet was hanging over us strongly. Now that the carpet is shifting and the sun is shinning it is not happy at all. It also liked it when the sea around was very hot because of the volcano, now that it's quiet, the monster is not comfortable. These favourable conditions are changing and so my grandpa said the monster is desperate.'

Bashir was not convinced that the monster would die a natural death when its time was up. He strongly believed that the children of Tatasi could kill the monster with their catapults and stones. Jamil did not argue further.

After about an hour with no sign of the monster, Jamil headed for the lake with Lucky, leaving Bashir behind. As they walked Jamil began to feel uneasy. He felt as if there was something in the air that was not right. He could not say what it was but he felt there was danger around. It was as if he was being watched. This was the first time he had experienced this feeling of insecurity and vulnerability and it worried him. He glanced around nervously hoping to see something. 'Lucky, let's go,' he commanded and began to run. As he ran he noticed his legs became weak and he slowed down and slumped on the ground. He felt dizzy. There was a strong smell around and the more he breathed in the more he felt dizzy. He started to cough and then vomit. His eyes closed. Strong winds began to blow around him. Jamil struggled and held on to a tree for support. There was still no noise at all and that baffled Jamil. There was another cloud of smoke that covered the area. He could hear Lucky bleating nearby but could not see his pet goat. Jamil began to suspect the monster was in the vicinity.

When Jamil managed to steady himself, he opened his eyes and what he saw horrified him. He saw a dark huge object emerge from the smoke. Looking closer, he noticed large greenish protruding eyes flashing red lights intermittently. What Jamil could see about ten metres away had a massive head, wide mouth with at least two tongues sticking out. This ugly beast started to move closer and closer still not making any noise. It appeared to be gliding. Jamil stood there and locked eyes with the monster. For about thirty seconds Jamil was eyeball to eyeball with the beast from the sea that had been terrorising the island. The monster looked straight at Jamil, sticking its tongues out and flashing its eyes. For the first time, it made a familiar noise – a grunt as it shook its head. It moved closer to Jamil and now stood about two metres away, still in a cloud of smoke but still possible for Jamil to see clearly. Jamil saw, through the smoke, something like a long arm pick Lucky from his side. The monster withdrew into the sea making the grunting noises Jamil had heard before and releasing smoke into the air. Jamil tried to look for his catapult but was too frightened and confused. He tried to run but could not. From where he was, Jamil could just make out Lucky being tossed into the air. Lucky was bleating desperately and loudly. Then silence. Jamil saw nothing after that because of the thick smoke in the sea. He feared the monster would come for him next and began to run.

After some time the wind eased and the smoke cleared.

Jamil hid behind a rock shaking and frightened. He looked round hoping to see Lucky emerge. There was silence. He began to look for Lucky, running around shouting, 'LUCKY, LUCKY, WHERE ARE YOU? LUCKY!'

Jamil was upset. He could not immediately accept that the monster had devoured his pet goat. He also found it hard to believe that he stood face to face with the monster. These two experiences touched and shook him. When he had recovered, Jamil stood up to go home, alone. He stood and looked at the sea.

'You'll pay the ultimate price,' Jamil shouted, addressing the monster that had since disappeared. 'I'll make sure you die a slow and painful death. I'll swim across to the other side. If you do indeed have a thousand mouths and a thousand hands, I need only one idea to get rid of you from the sea and free the people and the island. You have done enough damage and deserve to die soon.'

Somehow Jamil felt emboldened by the encounter. Over the next few days, he decided to trick the monster to its death. 'Face to face confrontation with what I saw is not possible. It's too big a monster and it'll be too risky. The monster will win in any one-to-one fight. I have to trick it somehow. I'll not discuss it with anyone else and do it alone. If I succeed the people will notice my absence and the death of the monster. If I fail, I'll be one of those that simply disappeared. Just another meal for the monster. Like poor Lucky.' Suddenly he had an idea, 'if the monster likes goats, then I'll use goats to kill it.'

Jamil secretly worked out a plan to trick and kill the monster. He called it the three-goat plan. He needed three goats, three boats, a long rope and lots of hope.

He decided to do a dry run. Since he chose to trick the monster at dawn, he set out one early morning with a goat to a place he had previously anchored a boat. He put the goat in the boat and pushed it into the sea. He withdrew and watched from a safe distance. Within a few minutes, he noticed the activities of the monster in the area. First the horrible smell filled the air, then thick smoke, followed by strong wind. Minutes later he heard from afar the groans and grunts of the monster. As Jamil expected, the goat was tossed into the air and then silence. This time Jamil did not see the monster; partly because it was dawn and partly because of the smoke.

Jamil spent several weeks perfecting his plan. 'The three goat plan will work,' he told himself several times. Sometimes he would close his eyes and simulate the whole process, in slow motion. He would start from the time he arrived at the harbour with three goats and go through the likely scenarios. He would picture several versions of the escape. When he was caught by the monster and tossed into the air and devoured; when he drowned; and when he swam across successfully.

On the eve of his planned escape, Jamil visited Bashir.

'The monster is in for a real surprise,' Bashir told him excitedly. 'One thousand stones all at once.' With his hand he demonstrated how the monster would be hit. 'I can see it groan and grunt to death and we'll dance and celebrate because my plan will succeed. I'll be seen as the hero of the island.'

'But the monster has no specific time and place. It attacked Lucky and I during the Monster Free Hours,' Jamil argued. 'Are you sure of your timing? What are you going to use to lure it to the specific place you want us to stand and aim from?'

'I'll get it right somehow,' Bashir answered then asked, 'Don't you want to be part of the history of the island? One of those who threw a stone at the monster?'

'Of course I'm ready to kill the monster,' Jamil replied calmly.

Later in the evening Jamil asked his grandfather a very leading question. 'Grandpa, do you think someone will swim across the sea one day?'

'Of course, if the time is right someone will succeed in doing it.'

'How?'

'Hard work and pure luck.'

'What do you mean?'

'If the person works hard at his plan and if it coincides with when the monster is sleeping.'

'But the monster never sleeps.'

'No one really knows its routine but if something will happen something else will make it happen.'

'Really?'

'Yes and it has happened before. Some people have successfully crossed the sea.'

'Why didn't the monster die?'

'Aha! These people looked back after they crossed. They didn't know that whoever crosses the sea must not look back at all. While the monster will appear dead, eye contact with the person who crossed the sea will bring the monster back to life.'

The next morning, Jamil woke up at the usual time. 'I'm going to defy the Monster Curfew Hours today.'

'Just take care,' advised Kamal. 'Now that you know how it looks and what it does before it attacks, you know when to take cover in a safe place.'

'Try to stay clear of the sea and the harbour okay,' Laila cautioned.

'Okay, I'll try,' Jamil assured his grandparents.

'Don't do silly things,' Laila cautioned further.

'Thank you and see you later,' Jamil said and walked away.

Jamil walked nervously to the harbour where he had the day before stored three goats and a very long rope in a shed. On his way, he cut a short branch of Tatasi plant which he tied to his waist. If he succeeded, it would be the only thing he would take from the island. At the harbour, he took the goats out and walked calmly to the points he had marked in his mind. From now on, Jamil told himself, it was maximum concentration. Everything must be as practiced. He put the first goat in a boat in the shallow area of the sea. He tied all the goats firmly – four legs and the neck to five points of the boat. 'This monster will have to work hard to untie them or will have to swallow the boat.' He then tied the first boat to the second one with the long rope. All this time, Jamil kept a nervous eye on the sea hoping that the monster would not attack.

When he was ready he released the first goat-in-a-boat bait into the water. 'Monster,' Jamil shouted into the early morning darkness as if the monster was listening or could understand him. 'I'm ready for you now. This is what it has come to. I'm ready for the fight. It's either you or me.'

Jamil looked round nervously. There was no sign of the monster. He pulled the boat back as it was drifting deep into the sea. He started all over again and waited. Still no monster. As time passed he became worried. Should he abandon his plans and return home? Should he just brave it and cross? Was the monster sleeping? 'Stick to your plans' an inner voice told him. He pulled the boat back and started all over again. 'Come on monster, come out and have fun. You love goats don't you?'

To his sheer delight Jamil noticed the familiar movement in the sea suggesting the monster was in the area. Just as planned the boat was also in the area he wanted it to be. 'Monster you are in for a good fight,' thought Jamil. His instinct told him that as long as he followed his plans, he would succeed. He ran to where the second goat-in-a-boat bait was and released it into the sea just at the designated place. He ran to the third boat very far away. Jamil stood for a second to be sure he was standing in the right place. He deliberately picked the point because it was the closest to the mainland. He hastily tied a small rope to his leg and the third boat. He pushed the goat-in-a-boat bait into the sea, looked at the island for the last time, took a deep breath and dived into the sea. As he began to swim, he looked at where the monster was and was glad that it was still struggling with the first goat. Jamil swam faster.

For some strange reason Jamil now began to ask himself, 'what if there is more than one monster? What if it really has a thousand hands? What if the monster comes for me instead of the second or third goat?' He did not answer the questions but kept on swimming. By the time the monster had finished with the first and was struggling with the second, Jamil was well passed the middle of the distance. But now he was getting tired. He had underestimated so many things, including the fact that the third boat tied to his leg would slow him down, and that the water was colder than he expected. He continued to swim regardless. He was determined to try his luck against the monster. He was excited because he knew the monster had fallen for his trick and the mere thought encouraged him to swim faster. He looked back and noticed that the monster was in the middle of the sea and was struggling with the second goat. 'Good,' he said and increased speed after releasing the third goat-in-a-boat. 'Everything is working according to plan.' The release of the third goat gave him the freedom he needed to swim faster. He looked back and was happy with the distance between himself and the monster. By now he could see the shore line ahead of him and knew that with a bit of luck and hard work he would make it. Jamil was so relieved when he noticed that the monster went for the third goat instead of him. 'Maybe the monster did not see me.' He continued to swim faster and faster. 'Catch me if you can,' he taunted the monster. By the time he looked back again he noticed that the monster had wasted no time with the third goat and was bearing down on him.

The monster's groans and cries began to get louder and louder – a sign that it was getting desperate. The wind was getting stronger which aided Jamil as it pushed him forward away from the monster. Jamil feared that the monster's long hand would snatch him any moment but he kept swimming hoping that he had enough distance. He swam faster and faster aided by the strong wind from the monster. The smoke from the monster was getting thicker too and was covering his eyes. The smell was strong but that did not bother Jamil. Through the smoke, smell and wind Jamil swam for his life and the freedom of the island. As soon as he reached the shore, he began to run as fast as he could in case the long hand of the monster pulled him back. After about fifty metres on the mainland Jamil collapsed on the sand out of exhaustion and lay there face down. He did not want to have any eye contact with the monster by accident. What if the monster was standing there waiting for eye contact? He pinched himself several times to be sure he was alive and that it was not a dream. 'Jamil, you just did it,' he said to himself.

In the meantime, the noise from the sea was becoming louder and louder. The wind was strong and the monster was splashing water all over the place. Jamil almost choked from the smoke and the smell the monster released but would not look back, or even look up. The smell was three times stronger than the one he experienced when Lucky was captured. The smoke burnt his eyes. The noise was so loud that he thought his eardrums would crack. He was determined to endure everything because he knew that it was only a matter of time before the monster would cease to exist. All he had to do was endure. His goal had been achieved and he was prepared to lie down there for as long as it would take for the monster to die. He was not in a hurry any more.

Jamil was sure he had won the battle but needed time to recover. He waited patiently in the thick smoke and horrible smell. After about an hour, the monster released the loudest noise he had ever heard. Jamil's body and eardrums shook violently. The noise pierced through almost every part of him. But Jamil was not scared. He laughed. 'This is the last cry of a dying monster,' he said to himself. Gradually the noise began to die down and with time it was all quiet. The wind and smoke died down too.

Jamil slowly opened his eyes. He imagined the monster dead in the sea or waiting on the shores right behind him hoping for him to look back. From the corners of his eyes, he made sure he was not facing the sea. He stood up – resisted the temptation to look back – and started to run towards the bushes. 'Monster I've won,' he screamed and jumped and danced but did not look back. He was proud of himself. Alone he had planned it and alone he had carried it out. That made his joy particularly intense. He chanted to himself:

'*Monster Monster you're dead*
Monster Monster you're dead.'

As he pushed into the forest, he could not believe what had just happened. It was like a dream. 'I tricked and killed the monster,' he screamed several times. The sentence echoed through the forest. It somehow pained him that he could not tell his grandparents how he had done it. Now he began to regret the decision not to tell them of his plans. He knew though that they would be able to figure it out that and that they would be happy with the thought that he was safe somewhere. He was happy the island was now free and the people liberated from the grip of the evil monster. Tears began to roll down his cheeks as he walked farther and farther into the forest realising that he might not see his grandparents ever again, he might not even see the island again!

CHAPTER SEVEN

Land of Mourners

Jamil was still in a triumphant mood as he walked through the forest with pride and confidence. Every step he took was a step away from the island and away from the monster. Away from what he loved and what he hated! Every step he took was a step towards his other goal: to recover the lost half-key.

The forest began to grow darker. Although he knew where he was coming from, Jamil had no idea where he was going to. He just kept walking. Like any other child growing up on the peninsula and then the island, he had dreamed of going to different places. He had never thought through what route to take once he crossed the sea. Now that he had done it, he was just glad with the feat and left the rest to fate. He had left behind a certain past, and now he faced an uncertain future.

Jamil continued to walk deep into the forest until it got so dark that he could hardly see where he was heading. As he walked he felt he was going down a slope. He wasn't sure but could not check as it was too dark to make sense of anything. He kept walking and felt more and more that he was going downwards, but he had no alternative but to keep walking into the deep darkness. Soon he reached a point that was completely dark. It was as if a sack had been pulled over his head. As he groped his way forwards, he could not be sure whether what he saw was real or imaginary. He thought he saw the faces of some human beings. The first one looked as if it was laughing at him but he heard no noise at all. The second face was crying with tears on her face but again Jamil did not hear any sound. Jamil thought the monster's noise must have damaged his eardrums. He continued to walk in terrible fear. The third face, that of a man, winked at him. As he walked he ignored other faces but screamed when he saw what resembled the monster shaking in front of him. He did not stop and walked past the figure. There was no sound, no smell, no smoke. He continued to walk into the unknown.

When there was a ray of sunlight, Jamil was relieved when he realised he had been in a tunnel. After five steps the darkness resumed with the same intensity. He did not see any other faces. He vowed that whatever he encountered he would never go back – that was not an option. He had only one path. Jamil continued walking in the tunnel and soon got so used to it that he almost began to enjoy it. Then there was light at the end of the tunnel. Jamil did not rush to get out. He took his time. When he did emerge he was hit by powerful sunlight. The heat was also unbearable. Jamil was stunned by the light and brightness everywhere, having grown so accustomed to the dark. He felt dizzy and had to close his eyes and rest.

Jamil began to sweat profusely. There were beads of sweat on his forehead, sweat under his armpits, sweat all over him. He tried to look up but his eyes hit the sun which proved too powerful. The vegetation was different. The air was different. The smell was different. With his eyes disabled by the sun, only his nose functioned properly. Whatever passed through his nose seemed too heavy for his lungs as he struggled to breathe, to adjust to the new environment.

After days and weeks of resting and walking in the wilderness, Jamil found himself at a crossroads. He waited there for three days wondering which way to turn. At last a man appeared and said, 'If you want to go to the Town of the Walking Eagles, turn left. It is a very interesting place but very far. If you want to go to the Town of the Angels, turn right. I'll not advise a young man like you to go there. If you want to go to the Land of Mourners, go straight, cross the river and turn right.'

Jamil chose to go to the Land of Mourners. 'I'm happy I'm on the path to where my grandfather came from,' he said, thanking the man.

The first person he met as he approached the Land of Mourners was an old man. He was wearing a long white rope and a small cap. His moustache and beard were grey. 'You must be Jamil,' the man said with respect and admiration all over his old but smooth face.

'Yes I am,' a shocked Jamil answered.

'We've heard about what you did and were hoping that you'd pass by this place.' He paused and smiled. 'The monster is dead and life is returning to normal on the island. Everyone on the island is proud of you.'

After days and weeks alone in the wilderness, Jamil was disoriented. The news that the monster was dead pleased him but he still found it hard to believe. 'Can people go about their daily lives without fear of the monster?' he asked.

'Jamil, the monster is dead. It died after you crossed the sea. The corpse floated on the sea until it was dragged and left to rot by the shores and its bones are hidden somewhere,' the old man disclosed further.

Jamil did not know what to say.

The man continued, 'I've met people who have been there. They said everyone knew you tricked the monster although no one seemed to know how. Some people said you flew high in the sky with something you invented, others said you swam deep in the sea.' Jamil could only laugh. 'I feel honoured that you chose to pass through this place. Your stars have guided you in the right direction and I really look forward to hearing your stories.'

They walked together until they reached a hamlet. The old man, whom everyone in the hamlet called Baba, gave Jamil a room in his house.

'I know you'll not be staying here for a long time,' Baba said, several days later. 'You have a future ahead of you and I'd like you to use this opportunity to learn from us. No knowledge is a waste, as we say here. Whatever you learn might help you in the future. It's not by accident you came here right after the duel with the monster. Everything in life has a purpose. I don't know what you intend to do but I know you'll not be here for too long.'

'You're right Baba, I'm just passing through. I've not decided what to do immediately as I never thought I'd be able to trick and kill the monster but I always dreamed of looking for the other half of the golden key and taking it back to the island.'

'What a great idea. The key is in Pashia Kingdom, in the imperial treasures of King Sacha. You are still young and have a whole life ahead of you; a life of adventure. Enjoy the journey to wherever life takes you. That's the most important thing. Preserve your life and, as you have shown by your encounter with the monster, learn to think on your feet. Life is not straightforward. You'll experience many diversions ...'

Jamil did not respond. He was beginning to feel unwell. He could not describe to himself what he was going through. There was a strange sensation all over his body. The old man noticed the change and asked him to rest. Jamil inexplicably became anxious. He put it down to fatigue and disorientation. He could not concentrate and as the time passed he felt something inside him was slowing his body down one part after the other. His eyelids suddenly became heavy. He felt dizzy and had difficulty in breathing. Jamil found it hard to connect with anything around him. All his joints ached and became stiff. Nothing in and around him seemed to be working and the more he struggled to understand what was going on, the more the feelings intensified.

First Jamil had the strange notion that the monster had injected him with its venomous saliva and this was a delayed reaction working its way through his body. Jamil came to accept that were this to be the case, he would be pleased to sacrifice his life knowing that the monster was dead and life had returned to normal on the island. 'After all I didn't win. It'll be a draw. That's fair.'

Jamil had never felt anything like this before. 'Why now? Why not earlier?' he asked himself. The next stage of the illness was very frightening. He felt cold all over and began to tremble. By now Jamil was resigned to the fact that the monster had got its revenge. He lay there in pain. He began to have visions – strong, wild visions that were hallucinatory. He began to see strange things like the volcano erupting, fire everywhere, floods, earthquakes, screaming and shouting. The most vivid was the scene where the monster chased and caught him. Just when he felt the monster grabbing him, his body began to shake violently, his teeth chattered and clattered and as his body shook he screamed, 'All right monster, it's enough! Why punish me? Just kill and eat me! Why do you enjoy seeing me suffer?'

Somehow he felt he heard the monster reply, 'You made me suffer for a long time too before I died. You too deserve a slow and painful death. I'll not do you a favour by just killing you. No. I'll make sure you suffer. I like hearing the anguish and cries of a suffering soul. When I'm happy you've suffered enough I'll devour you slowly. I'm not in a hurry. You think you are brave? You think you've escaped? You could have saved me by looking back but you didn't. You think you're very smart don't you? You didn't realise this monster has many lives. You only took one. It took me time to catch you because I wanted you to think you've won. Now it's my turn to deal with you. Revenge is sweet and I'm enjoying this one.'

Jamil continued to shake violently. He began to sweat profusely too. He slipped into a state of semi-consciousness where he felt nothing. After some time when he woke up he realised that the pain had eased. The body tremors had stopped. He was no longer sweating but was very weak.

'Are you all right?' he heard the voice of Baba. Jamil could not reply, he shook his head. Minutes later he struggled and uttered: 'I'm sick and dying. The monster is killing me slowly.'

Baba touched his forehead and looked closely at his eyes and tongue. He laughed. 'It's not the monster. You were bitten by an insect. I'll get you a particular medicine that will relieve the pain immediately. It's not the monster. It's a mosquito.' Jamil could not believe his ears. He still could not believe it wasn't the monster even though he was feeling better. He somehow thought the monster would resume the torture any minute.

'How could one insect bite have such an impact?' Jamil found it hard to believe the effects the bite had on him.

The old man gave him the medicine and told him to remain in bed for at least three days. 'Actually, you could have chewed the Tatasi branch and swallowed the liquid. That would have cured you,' he told Jamil.

'Why is this place called The Land of Mourners?' Jamil asked several days later when he had recovered from his illness.

Baba looked at Jamil and in a relaxed voice explained: 'First of all because we've one of the biggest cemeteries in the world. We've witnessed so many wars, so many deaths and so many destructions. Here we always keep an eye on death because it is ever present. The closest thing to us is death. There is a saying here that every step we take leads to the grave. We start with death to understand life. Every time we breathe in and out our death clock is ticking. I've seen so many things in life. I've seen the sunny and shady sides and I'm happy to have been blessed with good health. I'm happy to be in a state of tranquillity – no more rushing about – and I have learned to accept that there are things that are completely outside my powers. I'm grateful for everything now and have no fear of death though I still don't understand it. God is with me because it is to Him we shall all return,' Baba concluded.

Jamil was beginning to question his mission in life. Although he was determined to go all the way to Pashia to get the key, he could not explain why he suddenly felt the urge to return to the island. Soon he realised that he wanted to return to the island to tell his grandparents and the whole island how he had killed the monster, and to experience life on the island without the threat of the monster. He particularly wanted to boast to Bashir, 'I killed the monster before you.' He dreamed of a hero's welcome.

'What's there for you? Your dream was to travel round the world and get the key, so go on. You've done your duty to your island. You cannot achieve anything by returning home. The world is yours to explore and experience,' his inner voice stepped in.

Besides, Jamil was still secretly afraid of the monster. He felt that should he return to the island, the monster would come back to life and he feared he would have no chance against the monster in another fight.

When Jamil was ready to leave for Pashia Kingdom, he informed Baba, who after a long paused advised:

'Your life now is an adventure and a challenge. We do from time to time wander and get lost. It is normal. As humans we are made to go astray, to get lost in the wilderness, not knowing where we are and where we are going to. It's actually the easy part of life. The hardest is finding the right path. You are far away from home. You've just performed a great feat. Although Pashia Kingdom is your destination, the journey is the test and the reward. Enjoy it. It's not going to be easy but the adventure will be worthwhile.

'Life as an adventurer is full of challenges and pain and so face them with a big smile. A beautiful smile will see you through any challenge and pain. It's a remedy for success. Try to enjoy every moment in life. Know your life. Life is a journey and like most journeys it's impossible to avoid pain and discomfort. In most cases things don't work out as planned. In your travels remember that pain and suffering are part of the adventure. Wherever you are, wherever you find yourself – on top of the hill, in a river, desert – anywhere, there is a reason why you are there, so enjoy the moment, for tomorrow you might not be in that place. Remember that triumph is not just what you achieve but also what you avoid.

'I wish you a very good journey to places you've never seen. I hope and pray you meet the right people along the way. I hope there will be meaning in your life as you journey; that you'll know and find yourself.

'I hope you enjoyed your stay here and hope that your experiences will help you find whatever you are looking for in life.

'Lastly, forget about the monster and be prepared to have more pleasant things in life.'

After a year in the Land of Mourners, Jamil was ready to leave.

CHAPTER EIGHT

Where Women Are Leaders

'Just focus on where you want to go, not on your fears. If you fear, then you'll never do anything.' Baba's words rang in his ears as he set out that early morning. Jamil thought that whatever happened on the way, he would always aim for Pashia Kingdom and would try not to be distracted on the way.

To get to Pashia Kingdom, Jamil had two choices. Either he went to the north and from there crossed the desert, or he went south to the port of Orlonia and took a ship westwards. He chose the latter.

It was evening when Jamil arrived at the fishing port of Orlonia. From the moment he arrived, his instincts told him that it would not be an easy stay. The first people he met were not friendly. They cast suspicious glances at him. Jamil was taller than the average teenager in Orlonia. This marked him out. He tried to make friends but no one was interested. He wandered in the city till he got to the gates of the port where he saw a long queue and asked what it was for. 'If you want to work here, this is the queue you have to join,' someone told him. With nowhere else to go, Jamil joined it and sat there quietly.

'Life here is hard,' said the guy in front of him.

'What do you mean?' Jamil asked.

'It's difficult to get a job. Every boy wants to be on the ship these days and not enough ships go out to the sea. I've been here for days looking for other jobs but nothing.'

Jamil did not answer.

At dawn, Jamil noticed a very slow movement in the queue. 'That's it for today. They took only a very few men,' said the guy in front of him.

'Is it always like this? Very few people everyday?'

'Yes. One has to be very lucky to have a job on the ships despite all the dangers.'

'What sort of dangers?'

'Going to the sea is always dangerous. We've heard stories of ships not returning. Ships capsize in the sea. Some encounter problems. Sometimes there are fights and the weaker ones are thrown into the sea. Some captains are very brutal and they punish offenders by throwing them into the sea. So many problems on the high seas but that's the only work here.'

Jamil was not very sure whether to tell him about his dream of going to Pashia Kingdom. He decided to keep the dream to himself. He had noticed that apart from the boy in front of him, no one was talking freely. 'How many days do you think it'll take to get to the front of the queue?'

'Four or five days.'

Jamil waited in the queue for four more days. On the fifth day, the captain walked past the queue at dawn picking the boys he wanted for the ship.

'Hey you! Tall boy,' the captain said pointing at Jamil. 'You'll work as a fisherman for me. Follow me.'

Jamil was very happy to have a job at last. He obediently followed the captain to a boat called *Bermuda*.

'Does it go towards Pashia Kingdom?'

'Why did you ask?' questioned the captain.

'I want to go there in future.'

'No problem at all. We set sail at dawn and return at sunset. After about a month, we'll put you on a different boat that will take you westward to where you can take another boat to Pashia,' said the captain as he boarded the boat. It pleased Jamil that he would be working on a fishing boat and he looked forward to the experience. He believed what the captain said and from that day started counting the days before his eventual departure to Pashia Kingdom. He was happy with the routine of waking up and setting sail at dawn. He loved the early morning breeze and the smell of the sea. Sometimes he felt homesick as the sea reminded him of Tatasi Island. Jamil, though traumatised by the experience with the monster, did not fear the sea. Instead he liked it. He never had any visions of the monster while at sea.

Exactly thirty days after he started work on *Bermuda*, Jamil made an enquiry about his transfer to a bigger ship sailing westwards. He was told to be patient. He waited another month and was told to wait or sign up to a financial scheme that granted its members huge financial rewards which they could use to get a boat that journeyed westwards. Jamil did not think it through or suspect anything. He signed up to it because he was told everyone did.

With time Jamil realised that he had been duped into voluntarily signing up to work as a labourer on the ship for at least a year. Jamil could only claim the financial rewards after one year working on the ship. He could not understand why he had been duped and partly blamed himself. There was no get-out clause and should he attempt to run away from Orlonia, he would be severely punished. Jamil complained immediately and was transferred to another ship called *Destiny* which spent at least one year on the high seas. 'It's a form of prison. You're free to jump into the sea whenever you want freedom,' he was told.

The next day, Jamil boarded *Destiny* and waved goodbye to the port. 'See you all in a year's time,' he waved and shouted, just like the others on board. Jamil was not happy but could not show it. He did his best to hide his emotions as he had been told that any person that showed dissent would be thrown off the ship. He had heard stories of people being thrown overboard by colleagues. As the ship set sail, Jamil could only laugh at himself for choosing a route that would end with his dream drowning in the sea. Jamil was proud of liberating his island and people but here he was a slave on a fishing ship! But he did not feel sorry for himself. The words of his grandfather and those of Baba comforted him. He was beginning to accept that there are things that were outside his control. 'If I'm destined to go to Pashia, I'll get there,' he said to himself one day. 'This is one of those diversions in life.'

Three months after setting sail, Jamil woke up one morning feeling very uneasy. He could not say why. The sight of some clouds in the distance created a fear Jamil had never experienced before. 'Look at those clouds there? They don't look right to me,' Jamil said to another sailor.

'It's all right, we'll sail through. We have sailed through more dangerous clouds before and survived.'

'I have a strange feeling …' Jamil continued.

'No one is interested in your feelings, okay?' the sailor interrupted.

'Okay,' Jamil said looking at the clouds.

There was something ominous about the clouds and whenever Jamil looked at them he was nervous and anxious and would pace about on the deck of the ship. He was told in clear language when it became apparent he was restless: 'Once you're in the sea, you're in the hands of God. Just pray.'

Moments later *Destiny* was caught in a thunderstorm that raged for hours. It was as if the clouds decided to sail with the ship. The ship swung from side to side and they feared it would capsize and sink. When the thunderstorm subsided, the captain announced that the ship had been damaged and they would have to rely on the winds and mechanical power to take the ship back to port. In the meantime, strong winds were pushing the ship further adrift in a different direction. Five days after the thunderstorm, the ship was blown to a port in a place known as Fikkiland. Jamil's joy was clear for all to see but it was short-lived because the captain announced that they should all be prepared to spend years in detention for violating international law. 'Very few ships are released. The women believe any ship that mistakenly enters their territory is there to spy on them.'

Jamil found a place on deck and sat down looking disappointed and dejected. 'This is not fair. This was exactly one of the things I feared, that I'll not reach my destination. Here I am about to go to jail in a place I've never even heard of and no one knows for how long. This is not fair.' By the time Jamil had finished reflecting, smartly dressed female officers had boarded the ship and arrested all members of the crew. Jamil was handcuffed and led away for interrogation by an officer called Virva. She had a name badge on her chest. She left him in the room and walked out without saying a word. On the wall, Jamil noticed the portraits of Queen Sara and Princess Zara.

After about an hour Virva walked in. 'What's your name?' she asked in a soft voice.

'Jamil.'

'How old are you?'

'I'm seventeen years old.'

'Everybody is Jamil these days. How come Jamil is working as a spy?

'I'm not a spy.'

'Okay, where are you from?'

'From Tatasi Island.'

'This is not the place to crack jokes or make fun, okay? Everybody has heard about the Jamil from Tatasi Island. I ask because your curly hair and your height and shape show you are not from Orlonia.'

'I'm originally from Tatasi but worked on a ship in Orlonia.'

'I'm coming to that. According to intelligence reports, you people are mercenaries and spies sent to attack the legitimate government of Fikkiland.'

'I don't know anything about any plot. I'm just an ordinary person working to earn a living on a ship. I was on my way to Pashia Kingdom.'

'But Jamil the killer of the monster is not an ordinary person.' She stood up and touched his curly hair. 'Now tell me the truth or else I'll send you to the torture chamber where you'll be made to talk.'

'I'm honest.'

'Your captain was once detained here and we've found arms and ammunitions on board the ship. We suspect you people intend to attack us.'

'I am definitely not part of any plan.'

'For your information, your captain has confessed to charges of espionage. Whoever is found guilty will spend at least ten years' imprisonment or face a firing squad. The choice is yours,' Virva said firmly.

Jamil's mind went blank at the mention of a firing squad.

'If you are Jamil that tricked the monster, how did you end up on the ship?'

Jamil explained in detail what had happened to him. Virva was looking straight at him. 'I'll see what my boss has to say about the handsome boy with nice curly hair,' she said and walked out of the room.

Alone, Jamil closed his eyes and pictured himself being tied to a stake by a group of women even though he was protesting his innocence. He was afraid.

After about half-an-hour, the door opened and Virva came in with another woman officer who looked at Jamil closely for a few long minutes. She whispered to Virva and walked out. 'Her Royal Highness, Princess Zara of Fikkiland wants you to be her guest. I believe your story and you are a free person now.'

'You mean I'm free?'

'Not only are you free, you are now a guest of Princess Zara. Someone will come and take you to the palace soon. Welcome to Fikkiland,' Virva concluded.

Jamil could not understand such a sudden change. He sat there wondering if what he heard was true, but there was Virva, smiling freely at him, so he plucked up the courage to find out more.

'What is Fikkiland?' he asked.

'You mean you've never heard of it? Fikki means girls or women. Here women rule.'

'I don't understand.'

'Men do not hold political posts here. Men do not own land and huge properties. It is against the law. They receive very limited education as they spend most of their time either working on farms or working at home, so there is no need to educate them. Very few men are allowed into the armed forces and generally they are like second-class citizens here. They have separate quarters.'

'I see. Thanks.'

'Relax, Jamil. You'll not be treated like that. You are different. Princess Zara will give you preferential treatment.'

Jamil woke up the following morning in a spacious impeccably ordered room awash with sunlight. The room was in a palace that overlooked the ocean. When he had been brought there the night before, he had been too tired to notice anything. He had a shower and changed into new clothes given to him by palace aides. 'Her Royal Highness Princess Zara will meet you at noon in her office,' he was told after having his breakfast.

As he sat and waited in his room, Jamil shook his head in disbelief. 'What a life,' he thought, bemused. Although he was now a free person, there was something Jamil did not like about Fikkiland. He knew very little about the place and its people to make a judgement. He had had good experiences yet there was something that made him uncomfortable.

At noon, he was ushered into a wide office.

'Welcome to Fikkiland, my hero, Jamil the Great,' Princess Zara said with her soft voice and walked closer to him. Jamil stood there towering over the Princess whose head reached only to his shoulders. He could smell her perfume. Jamil did not know how to greet a Princess. He bowed but the Princess said, 'You don't have to do that. You're my hero. It's unbelievable that I'm standing in front of Jamil, the boy who killed the monster.' She paused. Still looking at him, she continued, 'what a voice you've got. It's a very deep voice. Look at his broad shoulders and his shiny curly hair.'

'I want to thank you very much for everything,' Jamil managed to say.

'Not at all. It's my pleasure. I've heard a lot about you and your conquest. I've always wanted to meet a courageous and intelligent person like you.' Princess Zara urged him to sit on the chair next to her table. She turned her young, smooth teenage face to Jamil who found it hard to look back. 'I hope you'll do for us what you did for your island.'

'I don't understand,' Jamil managed to say.

'You'll understand with time. I hope you'll be here for a long time.'

'Your Royal Highness, you probably don't know that I'm on my way to Pashia Kingdom,' Jamil insisted.

'I know that already. As my mother the queen says, we do not always arrive at the destination we set out for. Somewhere along the road we stop and in some cases these places become the new destination. Fate has brought you here so you might as well settle down in this place. You'll like it. There's everything, I mean, everything for you here. Just ask,' Princess Zara insisted.

Jamil was confused. He did not know what to say. He found it difficult to deal with the situation. He had no option but to accept the offer to stay. 'What else can I do?' he asked himself. But Jamil thought it would be better not to commit himself straight away as it would be difficult later to change the story.

'Your Royal Highness ...'

'Keep it simple, call me Princess Zara.'

'Princess Zara, I thank you for your offer but I'm on a journey and do not want to stay here longer than necessary. I promise to return once I get there and get what I want. At the moment, my mind is on Pashia Kingdom.'

'Take your time to rest here. You'll like it,' Princess Zara said. She walked to a corner of the office and brought a small well-decorated wooden box. 'This is for you.'

'Thank you Princess Zara, what is it?'

'Open it.'

Jamil opened the box carefully. 'It's the replica of the secret-of-the-heart charm bracelet. As you can see, there are twelve hand-crafted charms. The original, which my mother, Her Eminence Queen Sara of Fikkiland, gave to me on my sixteenth birthday last year, are the only jewelled eggs that are displayed and revered around the world. I've asked for her permission to give you a replica as a present because you are my hero.'

'Thanks, but why?'

'You're so special. I admire your courage. I want you to experience the opulence of this exquisite twenty-carat gold-plated bracelet. I hope you like it because it's the best present I could give anyone.'

'What do you want me to do with it?' Jamil asked.

'Keep it.'

'But I don't need something like this,' Jamil insisted.

Princess Zara was visibly angry. 'No honourable man rejects a present from a girl in Fikkiland, not a present like this, the symbol of something special from the imperial treasure. Any other man would have received it with two hands while on his knees and you cannot even appreciate it.'

'But Your Royal Highness, I didn't ask for this and didn't come for this.'

'It's an insult in Fikkiland for a man to reject a gift from a woman,' she retorted angrily. 'It's the worst insult.'

'I'm sorry. I don't know your customs, your culture, what is right and what is wrong. I apologise.'

'Why not stay and learn more about us?'

'But I don't want to stay …' Jamil replied with a raised voice.

'Listen to me Jamil,' the Princess interrupted firmly, pointing her finger at him. 'In Fikkiland, only the voices of Fikkis are heard, okay? When you talk to me lower your voice. It's bad manners to shout at a woman here and remember I'm the only Princess in Fikkiland.'

'I'm sorry again. But I have a dream and would like to continue my journey.'

'I have a dream too. In Fikkiland it's the dreams of the girls that supersede those of the boys. Just keep quiet and follow my instructions,' she ordered.

Jamil sat there in silence.

That night Jamil lay in bed with his eyes wide open. When he managed to close them and sleep, he thought he heard a clear voice:

'You set out to achieve a goal.
Resist the temptations to stay
Don't give up your dream
This is not a place for you.'

Jamil woke up. He could not tell whose voice it was but it did not matter to him anyway. Jamil's instinct told him that something was not right in Fikkiland for him. The next challenge was how to leave. He decided to bide his time. In the evening, Princess Zara, who behaved as if they had never had an argument the day before, took him to the centre of the old city. As they approached a stadium, he asked her, 'Princess Zara, what's going on?'

'We're about to watch a duel between two men,' she answered excitedly.

'Duel, why?'

'In Fikkiland whenever a man wants to marry a girl he must first fight another man.'

'I don't understand.'

'If a man wants to have a wife he must first prove his strength and loyalty by suffering and shedding tears and blood for her.'

'I still don't understand.'

'Here we believe a man that fights and wins a battle for our hearts will give the perfect happy ending we always seek in life,' Princess Zara explained.

Jamil struggled to understand the meaning of her words. So many things did not make sense to him in Fikkiland. He found it hard to fit into anything around him. He had no friends in the palace and lived a secluded life. As they settled in the royal box, Jamil was advised to sit behind Princess Zara. Jamil wondered for how long he'd live such a lonely life. 'This is not a place for me,' he said to himself.

As soon as the princess sat down, the packed stadium erupted in cheers. The stadium was filled with young girls holding paper trumpets, whistles and horns. There were screams of 'WHERE'S THE LUCKY GIRL?'

The referee entered the ring. Two muscular men in shorts carried a well-dressed girl on their shoulders into the ring. The girl waved. She was taken away. Then two men walked into the ring from two different corners. As soon as they approached the ring, almost everyone in the stadium except Jamil sang a popular song:

'Fight the fight of your life
Fight to show your strength
Fight to show your love

Show the world you're brave
Show the world you care
Show the world you're in love

Shed blood for the girl you love
Shed blood for everlasting love
Suffering is the twin of love.'

The two men – one in red and another in blue shorts – stood in the centre of the ring. The two muscular men paraded the girl again on their shoulders. After the introduction, one of the men shouted, 'She's the most important thing in my life. The only way this man can take her is over my dead body.'

There was a huge ovation.

'I'll certainly walk over your dead body arm in arm with this girl in a few minutes time,' responded the other contender.

The bell rang and the two men began to fight amid wild applause and noise.

Jamil sat detached and watched with amazement the way the audience screamed and shouted as the men hit each other mercilessly. Princess Zara was very excited. 'Bite him. Kick him where it hurts most,' he heard her shout several times. 'Finish him off,' she stood up shouting as the man in the red shorts punched his opponent. Eventually the man in the blue shorts surrendered. The whole stadium went wild with jubilation.

The girl was escorted into the ring again. 'I'm the happiest man in this world today,' said the victor with blood streaming from his eyes and mouth.

Jamil decided to plot his escape carefully, with no rush and no quick decisions he might later regret. He gave himself a week to come up with a convincing reason why the princess should allow him to leave. As he struggled to find a new idea, something he had not tried before, a guard told him that Princess Zara was waiting for him by the swimming pool. Jamil became nervous again. He had observed that meeting Princess Zara was becoming stressful and they ended up arguing, something he did not like.

'Whatever she says from now on, I'll remain as calm as possible. It's just a matter of time and I'll find a reason to get out of this place,' he thought as he followed the palace aide to the swimming pool.

Princess Zara was very forthright: 'I've been advised to let you go. You're free to continue your journey. It's very clear to everyone that you cannot fit into this environment and you are not happy here. I think you have so many things ahead of you and I don't want to be seen as blocking your path. I thought you'd like it here and settle down but I cannot force you. I hope that when you have realised your dream you'll remember us here. The bracelet I gave you will remind you of this place and the way we like you. Some people have told me that you'll come back to us in twelve years time. Each egg jewel represents a year you'll be away from us. I'm letting you go and will wait for twelve years. It'll be very special to meet you again when those years have passed. I hope by then you will have fulfilled your dream in Pashia Kingdom.

'I wish you good luck and forgive me if I've offended you in anyway.'

'Not at all Your Royal Highness,' Jamil started in a shaky voice. 'I'm very grateful for everything. But there is something I'd like to discuss…'

'What is it?' Princess Zara asked.

'The bracelet…the present,' Jamil stammered. 'I don't want to lose such a valuable present as life has taught me that anything can happen when one is on a journey.'

'I understand, Jamil. But I cannot take it back. Keep it. I don't mind if you lose it. I only wanted to give you something that'll add more colour to your life.'

'Thank you very much for your understanding.'

'You'll always remain my hero.'

CHAPTER NINE

Land of Crooks

'You're a brave person,' opined Nadir, the palace guard escorting Jamil to the edge of the desert, as they drove out of the palace the next day. Nadir was tall and lanky. He was wearing dark sunglasses. Jamil did not reply. He remained focused on his attempt to cross the desert. He had no fears at all. Unlike when he was leaving The Land of Mourners, Jamil was sure of himself. The experiences he had gained gave him the confidence he needed to continue his journey through the toughest route – the desert. Nadir repeated his earlier statement and this time around Jamil responded, 'Why do you say so?'

'It's one of the most dangerous routes.'

'It's the only route left for me.'

'Are you coming back?'

'Maybe. I'm not sure I'll cross the desert so I can't be sure I'll be back.'

'Princess Zara thinks you'll be back in twelve years.'

Jamil did not reply. The drive to the border post continued in silence. As they drove, Jamil began to feel different inside. He did not feel he was leaving something behind. There was no sense of loss. He looked forward to the challenge and was excited as the car pulled up to drop him. 'This is where I'm going to leave you. The oasis is not a long walk. You'll be able to get a camel and travel with a caravan today if you are lucky. You are such a courageous person. To leave Princess Zara and her wealth and choose this path shows tremendous courage. May you travel well. May you be guided and may your dreams come true,' said Nadir.

Jamil thanked him and alighted from the car. Nadir alighted from the car too. He gave Jamil a well-wrapped leather bag. 'This is from Princess Zara. She said it contains money and gold coins.'

'Please thank her for me. She has been very generous.'

'I will,' said Nadir looking closely at Jamil. Nadir removed the sunglasses and gave it to Jamil, 'This is all I can give you. You'll need it to cover your eyes against the sun and sand.'

'Thank you very much,' Jamil said and hugged him.

He walked steadily on the sandy path towards the oasis. He was happy with himself because he felt he was now back on his original path to get the key. 'I've tried the sea, it didn't work. I might as well try the desert,' he thought to himself.

At the oasis, under tall date trees, Jamil found a caravan ready to leave that had a spare camel. He used the money Princess Zara had given him to pay and mounted the camel.

As the journey progressed into the desert, Jamil's joy and happiness increased. He was beginning to enjoy the freedom he wanted. He was relishing the sense of going somewhere. This feeling of being on a mission filled him with energy. He felt the world was with him and he was in sync with the world. At last, here he was on a camel, turbaned to shield him from the sun and dust, heading towards Pashia. It did not matter anymore if he made it, it did not matter any more if they got lost, Jamil was happy and he could feel it inside him. He smiled as the camel continued slowly but surely into the desert. For the first time in a long time, he was beginning to believe in his dream again.

It took Jamil twenty-four days and nights to cross the desert. It was an endurance test.

'This time tomorrow, God willing, we shall be in the town called The Den,' said the leader of the caravan. 'It's the town closest to Pashiapolis outside the Pashia Kingdom. I suggest you disembark there and spend some time.'

'Why?' Jamil asked.

'First you need rest. You need to learn the tricks of Pashia Kingdom in The Den and not in Pashiapolis. You may not have the chance once you are there. It's always better to rest after a long journey, especially your first journey across the desert. If you really want the key, then learn the wrestling techniques in The Den, not in Pashiapolis,' the leader advised him earnestly. 'The people of The Den are very difficult. Don't visit them at night. Don't trust anyone there. Don't stay for too long. Never believe what they say. Not every smile is friendly,' the leader of the caravan counselled Jamil as they approached the town.

Jamil alighted from the camel very tired. He walked warily under a row of palm trees before walking on a busy road with street traders. He began to like it here. Maybe it was the noise or the way the people walked and talked freely. He felt at home. He was free at last to wander. He loved it because he was anonymous. The mere thought of not knowing where to sleep, or where to get food to eat, gave him the sense of adventure he always craved; the thrill he always wanted. As he walked on a bigger road with more stalls, he was shocked by the chaos. The street was crowded with wares and traders shouted and competed for customers.

As he walked along a particularly crowded street, Jamil noticed a boy of about thirteen–years-old walk into a stall and grab a purse from an old woman. The boy walked away calmly. The woman screamed and waved for help. She made eye contact with Jamil and something urged him to act. He did not think twice. He chased the boy and grabbed him. 'Give me the purse,' Jamil demanded in his deep voice, standing tall over the boy.

'That's none of your business,' the thief replied.

'It's wrong to steal.'

'But it's not your money.'

With a punch, Jamil forcefully retrieved the purse and returned it to the old woman.

'Thank you very much. That's all I've got in this world. Please sit down,' she said and offered him some fruits to eat. 'Where are you from? You must have just arrived?'

'I'm from a faraway island and yes, I've just arrived.'

'I could tell because you chased the boy and retrieved the purse. In The Den, these things are not considered wrong. Stealing is part of our lives. Please don't punch a thief in the future.'

'Why?'

'They can take you to court for hurting them. Here thieves have more rights than victims. It's not by accident that it is also called The Land of Crooks.'

The old woman, who gave her name as Hakuri, wanted to know more about Jamil.

'I'm just passing through this place to Pashia Kingdom to see if I can get the other half of the golden key. I want to take the key back to Tatasi Island where it belongs. I know it's difficult but I have to try.'

'King Sacha will never give the key away,' she said. 'Don't think that I'm discouraging you,' she paused and the tone of her voice changed. 'I hope you can get the key; hope you can defeat him somehow.' There was bitterness in her voice.

'Why?'

'It's personal. I'll tell you one day.' She waved at a man standing behind a stall across the road. He came over. 'This young man wants to go to Pashiapolis to get the golden key from King Sacha.'

The man's jaws dropped. 'What? The golden key from King Sacha? You must be mad,' he shouted as if stung by a bee. 'King Sacha will never part with the key.' He looked strangely at Jamil. 'Why do you want the key?'

'I'm from Tatasi Island and it is our property. It belongs to us, to the island.'

'I see. In that case you are not mad. You have a good reason.'

'I was told on my way that he sets tests to those who want to get the key.'

'That's right and he manipulates the results, that's why no one has ever passed the tests,' the man said laughing.

'What are the tests like?'

'No one knows. He decides, after all it is his kingdom. It could be wrestling or shooting or anything. Also, as you'll know when you get there, he's called the King of Beasts because he has chimeras; these are specially designed animals that he uses to kill those who challenge him. He once used the chimeras to kill someone who wanted to get the key. But don't worry, you wouldn't get that far.' Kolo, as the man was called, looked at Jamil closely and concluded. 'You'll never get the key. You don't look like someone who knows what he wants.' Jamil was hurt by the statement but decided not to show it. 'I cannot see someone like you outsmarting King Sacha in anything.'

The man's words were a huge blow to Jamil, but he kept quiet and just watched and listened. The more Kolo tried to convince him that he was not good enough for the tests, the more determined he was to prove the man wrong. But Jamil knew it would be wrong to state his mind openly. He had just arrived and wanted to know the people first before speaking out.

'The only thing you can do right now is work for me,' he thought he heard Kolo say. Jamil looked up to confirm if what he had heard was correct.

'What do you mean?' Jamil asked.

'Look after my shop for me. I'll be travelling next week and will need someone to look after the shop. My son does not want to do it. Maybe you'll be good as my shopkeeper.'

Jamil did not like the tone of Kolo's language and the way he addressed him but he decided to consider himself grateful for the offer of a job so soon after arriving.

'Take it. Work for him. I'm here to help you if you need any help. It'll be good for you,' Hakuri advised.

'It's just for some months while I'm away,' Kolo said. 'By the time I return you'll realise it's not worth chasing the dream. It's better to settle down here than proceed to Pashiapolis.'

'Okay, I'll take it,' Jamil agreed and he followed Kolo to the shop across the road to start work.

Jamil's work involved waking up as early as possible to arrange the produce nicely, keeping the area clean and smiling and chatting to passers-by to convince them to buy from him. Within a short time Jamil had memorised the prices, knew what was kept in the shade and what could be exposed to the sun. He knew the seasonal fruits and the price variations. He was also able to tell the difference between genuine shoppers and those he called time-wasters. Jamil was able to distinguish between real and counterfeit currencies. He was taught how to hide his takings in different areas of the shop just in case he was attacked by robbers and thieves. After a couple of weeks Jamil was left in charge of the stall. Either Kolo came in the evenings to collect the takings or he sent his son Yabo. This started well and progressed smoothly for Jamil. He was fed very well by Kolo's family and he slept in the shop. He started saving money for his journey to Pashiapolis.

'Ming, you must be finding life very difficult here,' said Hakuri starting a conversation one evening. Hakuri had advised him to take a local name so as to fit into the society better. She gave him the name Ming, which she said meant three things: the traveller who arrived at his destination; the man born under the lucky stars; and the man with lucky hands.

'It's okay. I hope to continue with my journey as soon as Kolo returns.'

'Sometimes life has a way of slowing us down or taking us away from our desired goal but don't be tempted to stay here for too long,' advised Hakuri.

'Yes. I think I'm getting closer to my dream and life has taught me to take things one at a time.'

'In pursuit of our dreams, we do go very far indeed,' Hakuri continued. 'I also came here with a dream of going to Pashiapolis. I also said once that I'll be here for some time but now I'm still here. Stuck. I arrived over fifteen years ago.'

'What happened?'

'I was very weak and fell for a temptation and I'm paying the price of an unfulfilled dream.'

'What were you going to Pashiapolis for?'

'It's a long story. When King Sacha's troops invaded the town called Rasmarat, he ordered that the first baby girl born under his rule be taken back to Pashiapolis for him to adopt. I was there with my daughter who, as fate will have it, gave birth to a baby girl the very next day. My daughter and grandaughter were forcefully taken away from me. After a few months, my daughter was sent back alone as King Sacha said he would like to bond with his adopted Princess.

'I was so angry that I decided to go to Pashiapolis to rescue her.

Looking back I should not have left home at all. When I reached here we heard the news that the girl had died after an illness. I was not sure whether to continue or return. In the meantime, I got stuck here. As you can see I'm old, sick and an invalid. And poor.'

'Can't you go back now?'

'I could but I have been postponing things since I gave up going to Pashiapolis. I always said next month will be my last and I've been saying this for more than ten years. I'm saying this because I want you to learn from my mistake. As soon as you have the money, just go. Don't wait for too long. Don't fall for any temptation here. This place has a way of making people stay longer than necessary. Go to Pashiapolis and try and get the key. Try and fail but don't fail to try. Unlike Kolo I actually think you could do it. If it's your destiny, you'll do it. Listen to me Ming, we all come into this world with our destiny written in our closed hands. Nothing will change what we came into this world with. It's all written on our palms before we were born.'

Later in the evening, on her way home, after closing her shop, Hakuri gave Jamil her parrot and an owl. 'They are for you,' she said in a voice that Jamil felt was different. Something touched him in the way she spoke. 'We do not reject gifts here,' Hakuri said, looking at the birds. 'Something inside me said I should give them to you. They'll keep you company. You can talk to the parrot.'

'You've just said I should leave ...'

'Ming, as I said, presents are not rejected here ...' Hakuri insisted.

'Thank you.'

'Let me tell you something Ming, since you came here I've felt something positive inside me. And such positive things happen rarely. I want you to succeed in life. There is a reason I gave you the name Ming.' Hakuri paused. 'Whatever you do please don't get yourself into debt. Don't gamble with anything. Be content with what you have and what you haven't got. Treat people with respect. Failure can be a success and finally try and see life as it is and not as you want it to be. Goodnight Ming.'

'Why are you restless?' Jamil asked the owl one night, a week after he was given the birds. 'I've been told you can be restless but what's wrong?'

'The big-eyed bird wants to show you something,' the parrot responded.

'Show me what?'

'What it can do with its eyes,' the parrot added.

'At this time of the night?'

'Actually, this is the best time.'

'Okay then. Go ahead.'

'Look over there, at the wall over there,' the parrot directed.

Jamil was intrigued when he saw some lights flickering in the dark on the wall. He stood up and walked closer. He saw clearly some moving images of scenes on the street. He could see himself standing by the stall and later images of himself serving a customer. Then there were also images of Jamil talking to Hakuri in her shop.

'What's going on?' a shocked Jamil asked.

'We just want to show you what the owl can do with its eyes.'

Three days later Jamil was serving a customer when he noticed a particular man trying to establish eye contact. The man passed in front of the shop again. He stopped and introduced himself to Jamil as a well-known magician. 'I'm in this part of town and thought I should call on you,' he said looking straight at Jamil. There was something in the man's eyes that made Jamil uncomfortable. 'Basically what I do is double people's money,' he started with a broad smile. 'I take a few notes like this,' he started to demonstrate with money he brought out of his pocket and covered with a green cloth, 'and there you go, it doubles in a matter of seconds.'

Jamil was captivated. The prospect of money increasing in quantity within a short time appealed to him. The man went on the verbal offensive. He didn't give Jamil the time to think.

'Almost everyone here knows and trusts me. I'm the man in

charge of people's prosperity in the market. You're new and don't know me yet. I've got an introductory offer for newcomers like you. With just a few hundred notes, I could double, treble and quadruple the money for you here and now and will not take any commission. This is a once-in-a-lifetime offer,' he paused and looked straight into Jamil's eyes again. 'You want money don't you? Listen, everybody here does it. It's legal. Actually, it's the only way people make money here. How do you think people get rich here? Selling fruits and vegetables? Everybody doubles their money in one way or another.'

As he spoke Jamil could hear somewhere in his head the voice of Hakuri warning him: 'Don't gamble. Don't trust anyone here. This is the land of crooks. People here lie through their teeth.'

Jamil summoned the courage to ask, 'If you can double money why do you need me? Why not take a note and keep doubling until you get a million?'

'Don't get me wrong, I'm here to help you. I'm doing you a favour. This is easy money. Do you want to be rich and happy? And quickly too? Do you know how long it'll take you to make the money I'll double for you in a minute?'

Jamil could not explain why but he felt a strange force directing him into the back of the shop, where he had secretly put his savings.

'STOP!' squawked the parrot. 'DON'T!'

Jamil stood for a second to gather his thoughts and walked back to the man.

'Sorry, I don't have enough money.'

'No amount is too small. Every little will help,' the man tried to persuade him.

'Come back tomorrow or later in the day,' Jamil argued.

'I'll not be here tomorrow. Why postpone till tomorrow what you can do here and now? I want to do it now. Just give me a chance to demonstrate to you how it works and you'll be convinced.'

Jamil shook his head in disagreement. The man moved closer looking serious now. 'I'm not here to play games, okay? Give me what you have made today and I'll double it for you, young man from a very far away island. You need money for your travels and I know you want to go to Pashia Kingdom, you need money and this is cheap and easy money. You'll be very rich and happy.'

Although Jamil was shocked the man knew about his plans to go to Pashia and where he came from, his mind flashed back to the financial scheme he signed up to in Orlonia and how he had vowed after the shipwreck never to engage in such things again. Luckily for Jamil, a customer wanted something and he had a chance to walk away. While serving the customer, he noticed Hakuri gesticulating at him. He interpreted her waving to mean 'No. Don't do it!' and when he returned to the magician, he decided he was not going to double his money. The magician was furious:

'You'll regret it. You are not going to Pashia Kingdom and if you want to see me later, then, you will certainly see me later.'

Hakuri later explained how the man was a well-known con-man and chose to visit Jamil because he was new. She explained that the man had counterfeit money hidden somewhere and exchanged the real currency for counterfeits. Jamil was happy he had stood his ground.

CHAPTER TEN

The Parrot and Owl Save Jamil

'All other things being equal, I'll be leaving The Den in a few days time,' Jamil told Hakuri that evening just before he locked his shop. 'Kolo is coming back tonight and I've made enough money to leave. I'm so pleased that everything went well. I will give the birds to Kolo's son if you don't mind.'

'I don't think he's the type of person that'll accept the birds. I'll tell you who to give them to when you are about to leave.'

That night Jamil was not ready for sleep immediately. He reviewed his life from Tatasi Island to The Den and was happy with where he was so far and what he had achieved. The difficulties on the way had taught him that chasing a dream is not as straightforward as he had once thought.

Jamil heard whispers at the door. Instinctively he knew something was not right. It was uncommon to hear conversations on the street at that time of the night. He closed his eyes hoping that the people would go away. They didn't. Instead moments later there were bangs. He stood up and went to the door. He could hear someone shout his name and recognised the voice to be that of Yabo, the son of Kolo, the shop owner. 'Something has happened to my father, open the door please.'

Without any hesitation, Jamil opened the door. A hard blow caught him on the face. He staggered back. Two blows hit him and he fell down. He was dragged into the shop and the door slammed shut. Someone kicked him while another hit him with a hard object. 'Hit him hard, especially his legs. He must not be able to run away,' said a voice he recognised as that of the magician.

'What do you want?' Jamil struggled to ask.

'Where is the money?' Kolo's son, Yabo shouted. 'Where do you keep the money? Give us all your money.' Yabo kicked him again and again. 'You think you're smart? This is The Den.'

The magician pulled him from the floor. Jamil felt something cold by his throat. He opened his dazed eyes. 'See this?' the magician showed him a sharp knife. 'If you don't cooperate, I'll finish you now and there are no witnesses.'

'I'll show you,' Jamil managed to say knowing he stood no chance fighting for his money. He gave them everything, all the money in the shop: the takings belonging to Kolo and all his savings. They grabbed it all and calmly walked away closing the door behind them.

Jamil was arrested in the morning. Before he was led away the owner Kolo accuse him of stagemanaging the robbery so as to have money to go to Pashia Kingdom. 'You've let me down and should expect a long term in prison.'

While in detention before trial, Jamil tried to understand why his journey had been so full of twists and turns. 'Maybe these twists and turns will eventually lead me to the key … Some days ago, I had everything: freedom, money and a big dream. I was very close to getting to my dream. Now all those things are gone. I don't mind losing the money. I can work after my release. I don't mind losing my freedom. But my dream! Could fate intervene now to make the impossible possible?'

Hakuri paid him a visit before the trial. She was very apologetic. 'Ming, I should have given you the job, not Kolo. I'll live to regret this for the rest of my life. I know you are honest and knew Yabo was a crook but it didn't occur to me he would do this to you. I should have realised on that day to be careful with the magician. I should have warned you that what he cannot steal during the day he steals at night. One thing you must not lose is hope. I had a very pleasant dream about you which I interpret to mean good news. You came here with good intentions and wonders await people with good intentions in their hearts.'

Jamil was formally charged with conspiracy to rob, deception, false information and stealing.

'Jamil has betrayed his employers, someone that trusted him with his business. Jamil has committed a very grave offence and must be punished,' emphasised the prosecuting officer. 'Let him suffer. Lock him up in a prison in the desert and throw the key away. Let the whole world forget about him there.'

The judge asked if Jamil had anything to say in his defence.

'I'm innocent. I deny all the charges. If I'd wanted to steal the money I could have run away before the owner of the shop returned. I waited for him so as to give him his money. I've never stolen anything in my life and urge you to free me,' Jamil pleaded. 'I was attacked by two men and they are both in court. One is Yabo and the other is his friend.'

'Are there any witnesses to substantiate your allegations that the two gentlemen attacked and robbed you?' the judge pressed further.

'It was late in the night and it was dark. I was attacked inside the shop and the door was closed. Only the owl and the parrot were in the shop when it happened,' Jamil said in defence.

'The birds are here,' shouted Hakuri. 'Believe me the parrot can speak. Please listen to what it has to say. Jamil deserves a fair trial. He's a very honest young man.'

'Okay parrot, can you tell us what you saw on the night of the robbery?' asked the Judge.

To the surprise of the court, the parrot narrated what it had seen, which corroborated Jamil's version of events.

'The parrot was Jamil's pet and like any obedient parrot it is simply repeating its owner's voice,' Kolo argued.

'Please give us one more chance,' pleaded the parrot. 'This evidence will prove to the whole world that Jamil is innocent.'

'What's the evidence?' the judge asked.

'The owl will show you,' the parrot said and urged the owl to show the world Jamil was innocent.

The Owl replayed the whole event in clear moving pictures – second by second – from the moment the door was opened till the time the two men walked away and closed the door. The audience in the court was astonished.

'We've nothing to add to what you have all seen. The pictures speak for themselves. Jamil is innocent,' Hakuri submitted.

The judge delivered his judgement. 'We cannot ignore what

we've just seen and heard from the birds. I hereby discharge and acquit Jamil of all the charges. I order he should be paid compensation for the injuries sustained during the robbery and be given all his money back.'

'You're free,' Hakuri said excitedly but Jamil stood there in disbelief.

'I just can't believe it!'

The old woman led him out of the court house. Kolo apologised for all the hardships his son had caused and promised to compensate for the injuries sustained during the robbery as ordered by the trial judge, and to return all the money owed. 'I want you to stay here and run the shop and others for me. You have proved to be very honest and reliable.'

The two birds flew and perched on Jamil's shoulders.

'Thank you very much. I owe my freedom to you both,' Jamil said smiling.

'That's all right,' said the parrot.

Jamil stayed with Hakuri for the next few days. For no good reason, Jamil had decided he had had enough and wanted to return to Tatasi Island.

'Whatever happens,' Hakuri said one evening, 'don't give up your dream. You'll live to see so many things. If you were able to trick the monster, survive the shipwreck, cross the desert and survive The Den, you'll survive and succeed in Pashiapolis. It's a place that tests everyone. If you are strong, you'll succeed, but if you are weak, it'll break you. It's not by chance that I call you Ming, the person born under lucky stars. You've been offended here but please don't be resentful towards us. You need peace within yourself to achieve your goal. You need peace within yourself to be able to wake up your luck, wherever it happens to be.'

Hakuri gave him his belongings and agreed to take the owl and parrot back. As he looked through his bag, he saw a piece of hand-woven multicoloured cloth about twice the size of his palm.

'What's this?' he asked.

'It's my present for you.'

'But what is it?'

'It's a long story. It was woven by my mother,' Hakuri said and started to wipe tears away from her eyes. 'When I was younger, I asked my mother to weave something special for me. Something I could use to tie my baby on my back. She gladly wove it for me and with time I proudly used it to secure my daughter. When King Sacha's army conquered the port where my daughter and her family lived, I was there to help her. It was that part of what I used to tie my grandaughter on my back when King Sacha's soldiers wanted to take her away. In the process of fighting the soldiers, the cloth tore into two pieces. My daughter took one piece to Pashiapolis while I kept this. My instincts tell me that it is this half that will lead me to the other half. One day I strongly believe the two will be joined together again and I'll be reunited with my grandaughter. My heart will continue to ache till I find the other half. I'm too old to continue the search for the other half. I'm not convinced that she's dead. I do believe that this cloth will help you in the realisation of your dream. It may not lead you to my grandaughter but might lead you to the key. If you find the other half, then that's your *Sudba*, your destiny.'

Jamil stood up to leave. 'I thank you very much for everything.'

'Please forgive, forget and forge ahead. It's the only way to succeed.'

'I will,'Jamil said.

'Promise me you'll come and say goodbye before my final journey?' Hakuri pleaded.

'I promise.'

CHAPTER ELEVEN

Jamil in Pashia Kingdom

As Jamil approached the massive gates of Pashiapolis, the capital city of Pashia Kingdom, he smiled and shook his head gently. 'At last,' he said to himself. Jamil stood for a long time in front of a big sign that read WELCOME TO PASHIA KINGDOM. It was written in white on a green background. 'Here I am, at last!' He was euphoric but could not show it. Jamil felt different: filled with a sense of accomplishment and of arrival. His whole body was relaxed. He had never felt like this before.

The first thing Jamil wanted to do was to make a friend who could help him round the ancient city of Pashiapolis. He had learned that to survive and succeed in a place like this he would need a friend; someone who knew the place very well. After all, this was where the key was and he must not make any mistakes here. He studied the people around the massive gates but no one seemed to pay attention to him. He greeted some cordially; others he smiled at. The people of Pashiapolis were very cordial and friendly. They responded but kept their distance. For three days and three nights, Jamil wandered through the city aimlessly. During the day he would walk around and at night he would sleep on a bench near the massive gates of the king's palace.

On the fourth day, as he approached the gates of Pashiapolis Park, he noticed a young man sitting on a bench and looking at him in friendly way. Jamil sensed the man would be willing to talk and walked towards him.

'I've seen you a few times in this area, are you lost?' the man asked Jamil.

'No I'm not, but I'm new here.'

'How are you today?'

'I'm fine,' Jamil answered sitting down on the bench. 'Are you from Pashiapolis?'

'No, but I know this place very well. And you?'

'Visiting.'

'Let's walk through the park,' the young man suggested. 'By the way, my name is Kojo.'

'Mine is Jamil.'

'Nice meeting you. This park is called The Four Seasons Park.' Jamil was happy to have someone to talk to at last. The two walked slowly through the huge gates towards the statue of His Majesty King Sacha. 'Total allegiance to the king is the first rule here,' Kojo said, looking straight into the eyes of Jamil. He was serious. 'Whatever you do, don't be seen or heard to be disloyal to His Majesty.'

'Thanks for the advice.'

'See the sign? It says: *King of Humans* and *King of Beasts*.'

Jamil nodded and asked: 'Why King of Beasts?

'There is a joke here that King Sacha is like a tiger. You never know when he's going to pounce on you,' disclosed Kojo laughing. 'Ah! Before I forget, whenever you hear someone say His Majesty King Sacha of Pashia, you must say *"May he rule over us for a long time"*.' Jamil did not ask why.

'We have the best queen in the world,' a smiling Kojo said, pointing at the statue of Queen Natasha. Next to the two statues was a big sign: *this is the eternal kingdom of fire and love*.

Jamil was so happy to talk after three days of silence. He was also happy that someone was explaining the rules to him. 'Do I have to say something like may she rule over us for a long time when I hear Queen Natasha mentioned?'

'No, you should say, *may her support for His Majesty be everlasting and strong*.'

After a short moment, Kojo said: 'You'll enjoy this place. I can see it in your eyes.' The two walked through a row of flowers. 'We like flowers here and in case you don't know, all these flowers are arranged to have particular effects. This place is well known for its flower therapy. I'm walking you through flowers that are supposed to make you happy and lighten your mood.' Jamil sneezed three times. 'Aha, that's a good sign. It means that Pashiapolis has accepted you and you'll have a successful stay here.'

Jamil was happy with his first friend. They both walked at a leisurely pace as Kojo introduced him to the culture and history of Pashia Kingdom in general, and Pashiapolis in particular.

'Where do you think I can get a job?' Jamil asked.

'There are so many jobs around for a young man like you but you have to have a work permit.'

'What's that?'

'Something that allows you to work.'

'How do I get that?'

'You have to have somewhere to live because the authorities will want your address.'

'But I've only just arrived.'

'That'll be difficult. Also, to obtain the permit you have to swear full allegiance to His Majesty King Sacha of Pashia.'

Jamil did not ask further questions. He thought that swearing an allegiance to be obedient might close the door to trying to get the key.

As they walked around the Flame of Eternal Fire – where pilgrims trooped to worship fire – Jamil's eyes settled on a particular girl. He could not say why, in the midst of hundreds of people, he should have chosen that one person. The girl, who was also looking at him, stopped and smiled. Jamil felt as if something had struck him. He looked at the girl again. She stood still with her eyes fixed on Jamil. Her gaze was very penetrating. It ran through his body like an electric current. He looked away but could not help looking back at her again and again. 'Is it an offence to have eye contact in a place like this?' Jamil asked Kojo.

'Why are you asking?'

'The girl there with the huge curly hair is looking at me and I'm not sure if looking back is offensive. See her? She's got some flowers in her hair and she's still looking at me and smiling.'

'I don't think it's an offence if she's looking at you. All I can say is that she's the daughter of a rich or influential person.'

'How do you know?'

'She's flanked by bodyguards.'

'Really?'

'See those guys in dark glasses by her side?'

'Yes.'

'They are bodyguards.'

'Why are there so many people here today?'

'We'll be celebrating King Sacha's birthday in two days time.'

Jamil avoided eye contact but could see from the corner of his eyes that the girl with huge curly hair was looking at him as she was ushered into a waiting car. Kojo left and Jamil was alone again. In the evening he had free food from a stall near the Flame of Eternal Fire. He returned to the bench he had made his temporary home. The picture of the girl with huge curly hair kept flashing into his mind. He tried to forget about her and concentrate on how he was going to survive in Pashiapolis. He could not. Her smiling face appeared in his mind whether he was sleeping, awake, walking or thinking. His head swam with visions of the girl. He wondered who she was and why she had stopped and looked at him. Her gaze was so penetrating that whenever he closed his eyes, he distinctively saw her gazing at him. He wondered what was in those eyes. That night Jamil dreamed of the girl. She had the golden key which she showed him and she asked him, 'Do you want it?' As he went to take it she disappeared into a thick smoke. In his dream Jamil stood for a moment and her voice sounded through the smoke: 'come and get it'. Jamil followed her into the smoke but hit a wall and fell. He woke up and looked around. It was dark and he was still sleeping on the bench in the square, near the gates of the palace.

The next day, on the eve of King Sacha's birthday celebrations, Jamil walked to the bank of the river Pashiapolis. There were benches there too and he could rest in the shade trying to figure out what to do with his days and how to fulfil his dream. The main problem for Jamil was how to get a job. He needed an address to register with the authorities but no one was willing to give him a job so that he could earn the money to pay for a place to live. He tried a few places and they all asked for a 'work permit'. As he sat there late in the afternoon, he noticed a yacht arrive at the bank of the river nearby and his heart almost stopped when he saw the girl with the huge curly hair emerge right in front of him surrounded by burly bodyguards. He sat there looking at her. She had two flowers in her hair and wore sunglasses. She recognised him, smiled and waved. He waved back anxiously. She stopped and spoke to one of her bodyguards. As the bodyguard walked towards Jamil, he was scared he had committed an offence and was about to be arrested. He wondered if he should run but he was weak with tiredness and hunger and did not know the city well. He stood up and waited anxiously. The bodyguard said:

'On the orders of Her Immaculate Highness Princess Asia of Pashia Kingdom, here are some vouchers for you to have free food at the palace gardens.' The man handed over some green and white vouchers. Jamil bowed to the girl, who smiled, waved and walked away.

Jamil was happy. He sat on the bench and smiled. He had seen the girl again and she had smiled and even waved at him. He looked at the vouchers, thinking, 'She even thought about my welfare.' Jamil experienced a kind of resurgence of energy. The mere thought of the girl made him happy. About an hour later, he walked to the gates of the palace and showed a guard the vouchers. 'I see you have a present from our benevolent king and queen who derive pleasure from feeding the poor and the needy,' said one of the guards and directed him to where he could get the food.

'*May he rule over us for a long time,*' Jamil said and walked into the palace gardens.

Jamil joined a queue. When it got to his turn, the same girl again emerged from a backroom wearing an apron and ready to serve.

'Hello stranger,' she said with a broad smile. 'You again!'

Jamil was too shocked to respond immediately. He did not reply. 'Are you hungry?' she asked, laughing.

'Yes,' he managed, avoiding eye contact.

'Are you really really hungry?' she asked laughing again.

'Yes, I'm really really hungry,' he forced himself to say smiling.

'What do you want to eat?'

'Whatever you give me.'

'I'll give you two portions,' she said. 'A big man like you should eat a lot.'

'I'm really hungry.'

As they spoke Jamil relaxed and lowered his defences. He felt he had known her for some time. There was an instant attraction, and in particular he liked her huge curly hair, her smile and her eyes.

'Thank you very much,' he said receiving the plate of food with two hands.

'Don't thank me, thank His Majesty King Sacha of Pashia.'

'*May he rule over us for a long time*. How I wish I could.'

'I can arrange a meeting for you to meet the king. It all depends on you,' the girl said as he walked away. Jamil did not pay attention to the statement. He was so hungry and pleased to have food to eat.

As he ate in silence, the girl joined him with a bottle of drink. 'This is good for you, especially if you are really tired. You look tired.'

Jamil thanked her. 'Who are you?' he asked.

'I'm a princess.'

Jamil almost choked. 'What? The daughter of Sacha?'

'Yes, but please always say King Sacha. It's an offence not to mention king before his name in his kingdom. Preferably His Majesty King Sacha. I don't want to see a handsome young man like you sent to jail.'

'His Majesty King Sacha of Pashia, *May he rule over us for a long time*,' Jamil said.

'I see you've been taught that already.'

Jamil felt elated. He could not believe his luck and his ears. He looked at her closely, thinking, 'Could it be true?' The Princess smiled and nodded as if saying, 'Yes, I'm the Princess.'

Jamil was visibly excited. He was also confused. He didn't know what to say. He smiled.

'Call me when you finish eating. In Pashia we always allow people to eat in peace. It's good for digestion,' she said and walked away stylishly. Jamil could not help but steal glances at her as she walked back to the serving area. He couldn't say what it was but there was something about her that touched him. Jamil felt he was dreaming.

After his meal, Princess Asia invited him for a walk. She looked relaxed and confident. She was full of happiness. She sang and skipped. As they walked on the lawns of the Grand Palace, Jamil noticed a form of unity in their steps. They looked at the same places, at each other and smiled and laughed at the same time. The princess was visibly excited. They went through a well-guarded gate into the inner lawns of the palace.

'What's your name?' Princess Asia asked after a long silence.

'Jamil.'

'What a lovely name. Where are you from?'

'From a faraway island.'

'Very far?'

'Very very far.'

'How did you get here then, if it is very far?'

'It's a long story.'

'What are you doing here?'

'Do you really want to know?'

'Yes. I want to know everything about you.'

'I'm an adventurer.'

'That's amazing. I've read so many adventure stories but I've never seen an adventurer before. I always wondered who they are and what they do. So you have a lot to tell me about yourself. You mean you go from place to place looking for something?'

'Yes.'

'What are you looking for here?'

'I'm not really sure. I don't know yet.' Jamil didn't want to tell her about the key.

The princess turned left and they stood in front of a four-storey stone palace with huge marble steps. It looked imposing. 'This is the grand palace of King Sacha of Pashia.'

'*May he rule over us for a long time,*' Jamil said and bowed.

'That's enough now. You don't have to say it every time.'

'But I don't want to commit an offence.'

'It's okay. I'm not going to report you.'

The two walked past an octagon-shaped hut with telescopes, chairs and tables. 'That's the King's Thinking Pad, as we call it. He's interested in astronomy and likes birdwatching.' They continued in silence until they reached an artificial lake with lilywhite flowers. 'This is Queen Natasha's Lake. She built it herself and personally arranged all the stones. She chose these fish and feeds them on a regular basis. She really likes this lake and the fishes.' After a pause Princess Asia added: 'My mother Queen Natasha has one of the best aquariums in the world. Very beautiful.'

'Where is it?'

'It's in the Palace of Harmony over there,' Princess Asia said pointing at the palace across the wide river. 'Queen Natasha likes painting a lot. One day, I'll show you all her paintings. They're beautiful. You'll like them.'

They walked past a herd of antelopes, a few horses and two peacocks.

'All this is beautiful,' Jamil was forced to say. He liked the symmetry of the gardens. He especially enjoyed the peace and tranquillity around the gardens with fountains in the middle.

'I thought you might as well know why it is often said that King Sacha is the King of Humans and King of Beasts. Here are the statues of fifteen chimeras that he has in the palace zoo.' Jamil was dumbfounded. He never thought they were real.

'You mean they are alive?'

'Yes and kept there. Don't worry they are well guarded. They are seen only once or twice a year.'

'I thought they were mythical figures.'

'No! I see them a lot because I play with them and can visit the area when I want.'

'Are they dangerous?'

'Of course they are.'

'Can I see them?'

'No, but they look exactly as in these statues,' she said, touching the first one in the row.

Jamil was shocked. 'Look at this! Head of a lion with a single horn in the middle of its head and long ears … oh my God, I've never seen anything like this!'

'Okay, let's go,' Princess Asia urged.

'Look at that one. It's got the head and wings of an eagle but has the legs of a kangaroo.'

'Okay, I think we'd better leave,' the princess said walking away from the statues. They turned round when they reached a sign: DANGER. NO ENTRY TO UNAUTHORISED PERSONS. ENTER AT YOUR OWN RISK!

Princess Asia walked away saying, 'Time to return to the kitchen and serve more people. As you know tomorrow is the king's birthday.' After a while she asked. 'Do you have any work here?'

'No. Do you have any work for me?'

'Yes, I can find you something. Do you like gardening?'

'I've never done it before but I'll do anything.'

'I'll get someone to teach you. I need a gardener right now. But I have to talk to King Sacha first.'

'Great. I'll see you tomorrow or the next day, or sometime after the celebrations.'

Princess Asia of Pashia was not in a hurry to go back and serve food on the lawns of the palace. She led him to a bench in front of another fountain. 'Tell me more about yourself.'

Jamil told her about his childhood in the peninsula, the earthquake, his pet goat Lucky and how he tricked and killed the monster. She listened with rapt attention. He was glad she had never heard the story. Then he went on to tell her about his stay in the Land of Mourners. She found it funny that an insect bite had almost killed him and laughed when he told her he had thought it was the monster. Jamil left out his stay in Where Women Are Leaders. He told her about how he crossed the desert; something she found very fascinating. She asked him a lot of questions, especially how he survived without water and how he coped with the heat. 'I want to do that too,' she said fingering her curly hair.

'Maybe one day, we'll do it together.'

'I don't think King Sacha will ever let me get out of his king-dom. Anyway, were you stung by the desert scorpion?'

'I wouldn't be here if I was stung by one. My remains would have been somewhere in the desert.'

'Where did you go to after crossing the desert?'

'I was at The Den and had a memorable stay.'

'How was it there?'

'Not bad.'

'I wish I could go there.'

'Why?'

'I don't know. I just feel drawn to the place. I just feel there is something for me there.'

'Please tell me more about yourself. I don't even know your real name,' Jamil said. 'I take it that Princess Asia is your official name.'

'That's right,' she said but her expression changed. She frowned, but as he looked at her she smiled. 'I'll tell you another time.'

'Why?'

'I've got to go soon. It's the king's birthday and I'm to sing at the birthday celebrations. I have a rehearsal today,' the princess said in defence but did not hurry to go. As they walked quietly towards the river, Jamil found it hard to concentrate. Too many things had happened within such a short time. At times it looked as if he was daydreaming. 'Look,' she tapped him on his shoulder and pointed to an enormous palace across the river. 'That's where I grew up. It's Queen Natasha's palace. It's called the Palace of Harmony. I know you have been to many places on earth and I haven't, but this is one of the most magnificent buildings in the world. King Sacha spent so much money on it. It took years to build and almost everything in there is the best.'

'And you grew up there?'

'Yes, I did. Queen Natasha loves water a lot. This is her official residence. She's got a palace by the sea for her holidays. The best for me is the one in the middle of a lake called The Floating Palace. That's the best. That's where I'll be singing next month.'

They reached a wooden bridge in silence. There were ducks

swimming in the river and birds flying above. The rays of the sun reflected on the flowing river. Jamil stood there enchanted by the sight. He looked at the birds, the duck and the sun and then at the princess.

'I cannot take you to my residence. It is part of the Palace of Harmony. I need permission from Queen Natasha.'

'That's fine,' Jamil said, still wondering if he was in a dreamland.

'Do you have anything to tell me before I go?' Princess Asia asked, avoiding eye contact.

'I've two questions. Why did you invite me into the grounds of the Grand Palace?'

'I like you. I like your voice, your hair, your height … everything about you. I felt something in me the first time I saw you at the Flame of Eternal Fire and then near the river. I don't know what but I'm at ease with you,' she said with honesty and clarity. 'And the second question?'

'Are you happy here?'

'Why did you ask?'

'You have everything, and the best too.'

'Yes I'm very happy but I feel something is missing. I like you because you have real life experiences; you have something you want to do with your life. I really like you as a friend because you have seen a lot and I believe everything you've told me. I don't know what but there is something missing …'

'What is your real name?'

'That's cheating. That's three questions not two,' she said, laughing.

'Okay, one more question,' Jamil said laughing too.

The princess frowned again. Jamil noticed her discomfort. She fingered her huge curly hair and thought for a while. 'Is it really important for you to know?'

'No but I just thought …'

'Okay, I'll tell you, but please don't tell anyone.'

'I promise.'

'It's a secret and as friends I hope we can trust each other with our secrets.'

'I promise not to tell anyone. I've just arrived and you are the only person I know here in Pashiapolis.'

'If you must know, my real name is Winta,' she whispered into his ears. 'My name is Winta … Wintana, but please don't call me by the name. I'll tell you more about myself later.' She looked round nervously. 'Jamil, why not give me a name? Call me by any name. I don't want you to call me Princess Asia. That's the name King Sacha gave me. Give me a name that only you will call me and only you know the meaning of,' she cried. Jamil was shocked to see tears rolling down her cheeks.

Jamil thought for a while as he tried to find an appropriate name. 'Okay, from now on I'll call you Haske.'

'Great!' she cried. She was so overcome she had to wipe tears from her face. 'I'm so happy I've got another name. "Haske",' she repeated. 'What a beautiful name. Thank you,' she said looking straight into his eyes. 'I'll tell the guards at the gate to get you a place to sleep,' she added.

'See you tomorrow, Haske.'

A week later Jamil was given a job as a gardener in the Palace of Harmony. He did not have to swear an oath of allegiance to King Sacha to get the job. He and Haske met from time to time to have a chat. Jamil did not tell her anything about the key. He thought it was too early to reveal the real purpose of his visit. Life had taught him to be economical with the truth sometimes. 'It'll be a grave error to tell someone from the palace that I'm interested in taking one of the prizes of the imperial treasures,' he said to himself.

Jamil also felt that Haske was withholding some vital information from him.

'Does the Queen approve of me sitting with you here?' Jamil asked one day.

'If she didn't you wouldn't be here,' Haske replied.

'What about His Majesty King Sacha?' Jamil asked further.

'He's away at the moment. He knows about you too. He's got spies all over the kingdom and my bodyguards report my movements directly to him everyday.'

'Is Queen Natasha happy we sit and talk?'

'Yes she's very happy indeed. She knows that we are only friends and she's happy I have someone to talk to even if that person is of a lower class and a foreigner. I'm allowed to talk only in public, okay?'

'And His Majesty King Sacha?'

'He's totally against you talking to me. He doesn't want us to meet at all and says he'll get rid of you one of these days. He thinks you are going to do something terrible to me. He said you came to his kingdom for something and if you don't get it you'll hurt him by taking me away. Is that true?'

'I'll not do anything to hurt you and if meeting you will cause any problems, I'm ready to stop. Also, if working for you will also cause problems for you I'll gladly find something somewhere else.'

'No! Please don't get me wrong. As long as we meet outside, where the bodyguards can see us, that's fine.'

'Okay, just tell me when it's becoming a problem and I'll leave Pashia.'

'I'll follow you to wherever you are going,' Haske insisted.

'What do you mean?' a surprised Jamil asked.

'I want to leave this place. I want to travel and see places with you. I want to see the world. The only place I go without eyes looking at me is the toilet and my bedroom. King Sacha keeps an eye on me all the time. I want to be free to see and experience the world.'

Jamil experienced turmoil after this conversation. He was not sure of what next to do. Should he tell her about his intention to get the key? If there were indeed tests to pass, what was wrong in attempting them? Jamil did not know what he wanted and whenever he reminded himself he wanted the key, he would feel that it was either the key or Haske. Sometimes Jamil would ask himself, 'Be honest with yourself, do you really want the key?' What he found troubling whenever he was calm enough to take stock of things was the way he was beginning to question his whole mission. Gradually, an idea started to creep into his head that obtaining the key was not really important anymore. The journey to

Pashiapolis was enough experience and even if he didn't get the key, what he had seen and experienced were enough.

The truth was Haske was beginning to occupy his thoughts more than the key. He became so confused that he wondered if she was a spy for King Sacha. Jamil thought that their meeting three times was not a coincidence. 'Things like this don't just happen.' King Sacha had been briefed in advance and he had sent Haske as bait for him. How else could he explain why she was not happy in the Palace of Harmony? 'She has everything, yet she claims she wants to travel with me. Look at me. What have I got? Nothing! I think King Sacha is behind all these strange meetings and ideas. Just to get me.'

Still Jamil could not deny that there was something in Haske that touched him. Her crying he knew could not have been planned. 'But there is something she's hiding from me,' he thought to himself. He was haunted for days by the tears rolling down her soft cheeks. Sometimes he felt like crying for her too.

In this state of turmoil, Jamil began to thank the monster. 'Had the monster not appeared I wouldn't have tricked it and embarked on an adventure. Were it not for the monster, I wouldn't be here. I wouldn't have met Haske! Thank you monster!'

'Imperial protocols demand that you bow down when you appear before His Majesty King Sacha of Pashia,' a palace aide briefed Jamil in a room at the palace. Two palace guards escorted him slowly into the private chambers where King Sacha, Queen Natasha and Princess Asia were waiting. Jamil walked carefully on the handwoven carpets. There were different types of mirrors on the walls with delicate plaster carvings. There were vases, flowers, swords, books and artworks on the walls of the private chambers.

'Your Majesty the King of Pashia, *the king of humans and the king of beasts*, Jamil is here to greet you,' the palace aide announced.

'Good afternoon, Your Majesty King Sacha of Pashia, *may you rule over us for a long time*,' Jamil said with a bow.

With a very broad smile, King Sacha responded from his huge throne, 'Good afternoon Wonderboy from Tatasi Island.' Jamil was shocked to hear the king mention the island. 'Welcome to my kingdom the boy who killed the monster and saved his island by flying over the sea. My beloved daughter, the diamond of Pashia, Princess Immaculate, the most precious thing I have in this world, has said so many interesting things about you,' the king said leaning forward. 'Even before she told me anything about you, my emissaries reported so many things about you. I know who you are and what you came here for.'

King Sacha struggled to get down from the throne. An aide helped him and he sat down next to Jamil on a long sofa. 'Old age is not fun,' he grumbled. 'Not even for a king.' He asked the aide to massage his aching back. 'Wonderboy,' King Sacha turned to Jamil, 'we have flowers that can cure anything except old age, stupidity and death.'

Jamil was not comfortable sitting next to King Sacha. It was a strange experience. 'So this is what a king looks like?' he said to himself as he studied the king's facial features. Jamil was overwhelmed by the sight of the king sitting next to him.

'I'm very pleased to meet you at last,' King Sacha said after the aide had finished massaging his back. 'I like tough people; people who achieve things. I suppose since you've tricked and killed the monster and made it all the way here, the ultimate challenge is getting the other half of the golden key.'

Jamil did not expect such a statement. He was unprepared and didn't know how to respond. He stammered, 'Your Majesty, I don't know what I want.'

'You certainly did not come here for fun. You have a clear mission. People like you don't just visit. The path you are on in life leads you straight to the key. I know that already and I'm prepared too. Remember I'm officially the Guardian of the Golden Key of Tatasi. So many people have tried and failed to get the key.' King Sacha paused and looked at Jamil for a few seconds. 'Have you sworn the oath of allegiance to the crown yet?

'No,' Jamil answered.

'That's good because if you had sworn the oath of allegiance, you cannot fight for the key.'

'Is it possible for me to just see it? I'd be content with just seeing and, if allowed, touching it, Your Majesty King of Pashia.'

'Of course you can see it,' King Sacha said with a shrug. 'Bring the key.'

Two palace guards walked in with a wooden box and brought out a key. 'Let him touch it. Let him hold it,' King Sacha said lightly.

Jamil could not believe his eyes and his luck. What he had thought was unattainable some months ago was right in front of him. There he was touching the key without any effort. 'It's definitely different from the one we used to carry in Tatasi. It's different from the one I saw at close range during the official opening of the new palace. It is shorter, older, thicker and more authentic. There is something special about this key.' There was something else that made the key different that Jamil could not immediately describe. 'Incredible! This is the Gift from the Heavens which means a lot to the people of Tatasi but is just an artefact here in Pashiapolis,' Jamil said to himself. The more Jamil looked at it the more it seemed to hypnotise him into fighting for it. He struggled with his emotions. 'This key does not belong here. It should be returned to its rightful place and I will do my best to get it back,' he thought.

Jamil returned the key to the guards and thanked the king for letting him touch it.

'Are you ready to fight for the key?'

'No Your Majesty,' Jamil replied.

'What?' King Sacha shouted. 'You come all the way from Tatasi for something and then give up? What sort of a man are you? I'd be very disappointed if you gave up as I thought you'd be a good fighter.'

'There are many things this lovely young man can do with

himself here,' Queen Natasha said, joining the conversation. 'He can study, work or join the army.'

'Certainly not the army,' King Sacha objected loudly.

'He's got a decent head on his shoulders,' Queen Natasha countered.

'That he has to prove, and the best way to prove he's got something in his head is to fight for the key. This is what brought him to my kingdom. He cannot just come and change his mind and do something else. No way!'

'You men always talk about fighting,' Queen Natasha said.

'Of course we have to fight to show we are men,' King Sacha replied smiling.

The King and Queen of Pashia Kingdom started to argue. Haske sat quietly.

Jamil was not sure if he wanted the key anymore. 'Does anyone on the island know that I'm here? No. Does anyone on the island care about the key? I'm not sure. Does anyone want the key? No. Does the island need it now? No. Is it relevant now that it is an island? Maybe. Since no one has won any of the fights before, do I have a chance? No.'

Jamil sat there trying hard to convince himself that the new island did not need the old key that was sent to the place when it was a peninsula. 'Why should I fight for something that might not be useful anyway?'

Jamil seemed content with seeing and touching the golden key. He was not in the mood to fight anymore. He tried to find a reason. He thought he had travelled long enough and he lacked the confidence to fight. The king would not let it go so why bother? Jamil felt he had done his share for the island and it was time he did something else.

Jamil looked at Haske from the corner of his eyes. Meeting her brought out something in him that no other person had done before; not even his parents and grandparents. He found in her a strong person who was familiar to him; who was interested in him. Ever since they first met he could close his eyes and remember every step she took, every blink of the eye, every fold of her skin, every smile and every curl of her huge hair. Everything about her was deep in his memory. Jamil had noticed that he had considerably changed since he came to Pashiapolis. He felt somehow settled. He was full of joy, excitement and confidence, especially whenever he thought about Haske or was with her.

Consciously or unconsciously Jamil had been questioning his priorities. He would never have believed that anything could compete for his attention and overwhelm him the way Haske had done. As she sat there, on a chair opposite him fingering her curly hair, Jamil stole glances at her. Haske was like a full moon that eclipsed everything in his life. Maybe that was why he gave her the name Haske, which means light in the Tatasi language. She had illuminated his life. She had added so many positive things that he felt his path was brighter whenever he thought about her. He looked at her again. She noticed it and looked at him too and smiled. Did he really want to leave her and go and fight for the key? It was a stark choice: the key or Haske. He thought, Jamil you cannot have both!

CHAPTER TWELVE

Fighting the Chimeras

Several days later, Haske's laughter could be heard from afar on the well-lit lawns of the king's Grand Palace one night. Walking under the full moon, Jamil was telling Haske more about his experiences in Where Women Are Leaders. What made her laugh was the duel between two men before they can marry a woman. 'Now I know why you didn't stay there. You were a coward. I wish King Sacha would introduce it here too. I agree with the women there. Boys and men must fight.'

'I'm not a coward. I had a goal ahead of me and didn't feel like settling down there. If I'd fought and won, I wouldn't be here with you. If I had lost, I could have been anywhere, but not here,' Jamil explained calmly.

There was a long period of silence.

'What are you thinking about?' Haske asked as they passed under a lamp.

'Many things.'

'Lucky you. You have many things to think about.'

'Many things to worry about.'

'Like what?'

'The tests for the key. Why do you think King Sacha is taking his time to decide when I'll do the tests?'

'He's the king and you are in his kingdom. Simple. He has the time. You want the key, so you have to be patient. Why are you in a hurry?'

'I'm not. It's just very frustrating. Do you think it's deliberate?'

'No! He's just like that.'

As they approached another lamp, Jamil turned to face Haske, stopped and admitted: 'To be honest Haske, I don't want to fight or do any test for the key any more. I have given up the whole idea and would like to inform His Majesty King Sacha of Pashia as soon as possible. I think I've done my duty to the island and I want to leave the key. I have other things I want to do with my life.'

Haske was shocked. She stood there with her mouth wide open. 'You cannot be serious!'

Jamil was confused because he had expected Haske to agree with him. He thought they were on the same wavelength. 'I'm serious. I've given up.'

'Why?'

'I don't know why.'

'You must have a reason.'

'Okay, I've many reasons.'

'What are they?'

'I don't think I stand a chance of getting it.'

'That's not an excuse.'

'King Sacha will get rid of me one way or the other.'

'So! What are you talking about?'

Jamil paused. He knew Haske was looking at him but he avoided eye contact. With his head bowed he continued, 'Haske, I'll soon be twenty years old. I left Tatasi when I was about four-teen … It's true I've come a long way for the golden key but my priorities have changed.'

'I still don't get it,' Haske insisted, walking closer to him.

'I'm thinking seriously about my future. If I'm banished by King Sacha where will I go? What will I do? What life would I have after leaving this place? What if fighting for the key directly or indirectly hurts you. You're the last person I want to see hurt,' Jamil tried to explain, getting agitated. 'Don't get me wrong, I am as determined inside as ever to get the key but I don't want to lose you in the process. Do you understand now?'

'No. I don't understand,' Haske said. 'Jamil, look straight into my eyes. What's going on with you? What's going on inside your head? You came all the way from Tatasi for something and now that it is within your reach, you give up? The golden key is about fifty metres from here, fifty metres from you … it's just over there in the Grand Palace and you give up? I cannot understand this.

What if I'm not hurt? I didn't know you were so weak. I always admired your courage and bravery and now you want to walk away from the biggest challenge of your life.'

'You don't understand Haske,' Jamil tried to explain, still avoiding eye contact. 'I'm not weak. What if my luck runs out? What if I lose? What if the king banishes me?'

'So what?'

'I'm not a coward. I just don't want to lose you, okay? What if you and I are separated in the quest for the key. I could lose both you and the key. I'm thinking about you!' Jamil tried to explain that he had the strength and belief in himself but the terrifying thought of losing Haske was what was bothering him.

'I see. So it's all about me. I didn't realise I'm that important to you,' Haske said. 'But we are just friends. Don't worry about me. Nothing should distract you from your goal in life.'

Jamil looked at her intently. She continued calmly in her soft voice. 'Listen Jamil, if we're destined to be together in future, we'll be together. Nothing will stop it from happening. If we're not destined to be together, fight or no fight, key or no key, King Sacha or no King Sacha, nothing will bring us together. Okay?'

'Think about the worst case scenario, Haske. King Sacha might just send me to fight the chimeras,' Jamil said, his voice getting louder.

'Why are you so agitated? Calm down. When we get to the problem, we'll find a solution.'

'How do you defeat a chimera?'

'Don't shout! Calm down.'

'But Haske, how do you defeat a chimera?' Jamil repeated the question.

'As King Sacha says, every man has a beast inside him. Time to show yours. Simple!' Haske said walking away slowly. 'Why are you afraid? Have you lost your bravery?'

'No I haven't but I don't know what to do.'

'You know perfectly well what to do. You're just confused,' she paused. 'Did you look at the monster and say it's too frightening to trick it?'

'No, I didn't, but ...'

'No *buts* here. But what?'

'I don't want to die here fighting for a key that might not be of use to the island. I want to do something useful with my life.'

'If you didn't die tricking the monster, you won't die fighting the chimeras – that is if King Sacha says you should fight them. Jamil, it's a question of honour and you must be strong. Promise me you'll change your attitude. You have to be positive to be a winner.'

'I promise.'

'Are you happy here?' Queen Natasha asked Jamil one afternoon while they were waiting in the dining room in the palace. 'My daughter thinks you've been unhappy of late,' she said with a genuinely concerned face.

'Not really,' Jamil said smiling and looking at Haske who was casting nervous glances at Queen Natasha.

'I can understand your frustration because the king is taking such a long time to decide. You must be patient. Unfortunately I cannot influence the king on such matters. He's the king and his decisions are final in his kingdom.' There was a short period of silence. 'I'm really worried about you,' Queen Natasha resumed with her sympathetic face. 'Do you intend to return to the island or do you want to settle down here?'

'It depends on many things.'

'Like what?'

'Like what His Majesty decides. Of course if His Majesty King Sacha banishes me from his kingdom then I'll have to return to the island. I told Her Immaculate Highness Princess Asia that I no longer feel so strongly about returning the key to Tatasi,' Jamil answered stealing glances at Haske.

'I can understand what's going on in your mind, but you set out for it. You must be missing the island now. You've been away for such a long time.'

'Yes but I'm not really eager to go back to the island. I've been away for such a long time and I've seen and touched the key which was a goal fulfilled. It's enough and I'm satisfied.'

'There is a Pashia saying: to be a guest is good, but home is best.'

King Sacha entered the dinning room smiling.

'May you rule over us for a long time,' said Jamil and he stood up and bowed down in reverence.

'Wonderboy, what are you doing with yourself these days?' King Sacha asked sitting down.

'Nothing Your Majesty.'

'He's thinking of returning to the island without the key,' Queen Natasha disclosed.

'No way! You came to my kingdom with the intention of getting the key. It's too late to pull out now. As you know I make the rules.'

They ate in silence.

'Would you like something else?' Queen Natasha asked with a broad smile. 'Eat. You need a lot of food. You are young and you ought to be strong.'

'What's going on here?' King Sacha asked with a frown. 'Do you want him to defeat me in a fight? Is there a conspiracy here?'

'You're too old to fight a young man like this,' Queen Natasha laughed.

'Wonderboy, when I was young and strong, I was the best wrestler around. My back never touched the ground. That's why I was called Prince Sacha the Cat. Even when I became a king no one defeated me.'

'But you cannot fight now,' responded Queen Natasha.

'Yes, I've got a bad back. I have an idea, since I cannot fight him, I'll get him to wrestle the champion of the kingdom called Dangerous Dragon. He's very brutal. He'll finish Jamil in two seconds. He'll break your bones into pieces.'

'No we don't need all this show of strength anymore. Let him eat in peace. Just give him the key and let him return to the island in one piece,' Queen Natasha was getting angry. 'He has suffered enough in life. Imagine what he's been through and now you want him to face Dangerous Dragon.'

King Sacha ignored the queen. 'For the first time in my life, I'll fail to wrestle someone who wants the key.'

'That's a good omen for you Jamil,' Queen Natasha murmured.

King Sacha looked at Jamil and muttered something like: 'he has to prove he's got a decent head on his shoulders.' He looked at the Princess. 'You know what?' His expression changed as his eyes settled on Jamil. 'Lucky should have been your real name.' He did not explain why but fixed his eyes on Jamil for a while. King Sacha looked at his daughter then turned to Jamil. 'Okay, your first test for the key will be an intellectual one – to prove you've got a decent head on your shoulders. You'll read sixty books covering major subjects from algebra to zoology and will be tested by a panel of learned judges. This will be done in six months. No extension.'

'As it pleases Your Majesty. *May you rule over us for a long time,*' said Jamil.

'If you pass you'll be given the King's Gold Medal,' King Sacha disclosed.

'And he gets the key and can return to the island,' Queen Natasha interjected.

'No,' said King Sacha. 'It doesn't work like that. If he fails (and I expect him to do so), he'll be banished from my kingdom. If he passes he will still have to fight to get the key. You have to remember that my troops fought to get the key from a neighbouring state and whoever wants to take it must fight too. The Tatasians did not present it to me in a ceremony so I'm not going to give it to Jamil without a fight. Simple.' King Sacha rose to his feet. 'The key is one of the most important pieces in the imperial treasury and as Guardian of the Golden Key, I'll use every means necessary to defend and keep it in my kingdom. If you want gold, you have to dig deep into the earth. If you want pearls you have to go to the bottom of the sea. If you want the key, you have to pass some tough tests. There is no shortcut to getting the key. By the way, I'm not going to make it easy for the wonderboy. He has to prove to me that he is a wonderboy.'

'Okay, can we have it on record he's not going to face the chimeras or the Dangerous Dragon?' Queen Natasha suggested.

'I cannot guarantee anything. I don't know what the test will be. It depends on my mood.'

'Now we'll see what your brain is made of,' Haske teased Jamil.

'I'm so relieved I don't have to fight either the Dangerous Dragon or the chimeras,' he replied.

Jamil was taken to the Imperial Institute for Advanced Learning where he was given all the books and an apartment where he could prepare for the test. 'How does King Sacha expect me to read and understand all these in six months?' Jamil asked himself as he fingered the books in his room. 'It's impossible.'

That night, Jamil listened to his inner voice: 'never say it's impossible. You have to try and see. You've come far for this key and every problem has an answer. You have to look for the way out. You have to show King Sacha that you have the intelligence to pass the examination. You must show Haske you can do it. How could you stand and look into her eyes and say "I cannot do it"? Imagine the shame!'

At dawn, Jamil woke up with a plan. He would try speed reading. 'Lying in bed will not put knowledge into my head. I might as well try it.' Jamil tried speed reading and to his surprise he read many pages during the day. In the evening, while trying to summarise what he had learned, he decided to read aloud so as to hear his voice and memorise the main points. Jamil found a bronze bust of King Sacha in his apartment and started to read to it. 'I'll read it to you,' he said, 'and I will remember. I'll use you to advance my knowledge and get the key.'

Jamil surprised himself with his ability to read and memorise the information within a very short period of time. He finished the books and had time to revise before the examinations.

When the six month period was up, Jamil was taken to the Grand Hall of Knowledge and Understanding on King Sacha

Hills, where he was to be tested by members of the Imperial Learned Council. In the waiting hall, Jamil remembered the words of Haske over six months ago. 'King Sacha will not send you to fight the chimeras. He only sends criminals and saboteurs and especially those who violate the oath of allegiance to the crown. You have not taken that oath and should not worry. The worst he will do is banish you from his kingdom. I'll do all I can for you to get the key so that the two of us can return to the island and live happily ever after.'

Jamil was ushered into a massive hall. 'Please sit down,' said the chairman of the Imperial Learned Council. He introduced Jamil, the panel, the medal and the procedure. Jamil sat on a thick black leather chair facing the panel. He looked round nervously. His eyes met those of Haske who waved at him. He simply nodded back, but he had noticed her new hairstyle.

'Our first subject is algebra,' announced the chairman.

The question and answer session took over three hours. Jamil was grilled on all subjects. He was happy he answered almost all of them and was very pleased with himself when the judges retired to decide.

Moments later the judges returned. The chairman delivered a long speech praising Jamil and concluded: 'We unanimously conclude that you have passed with distinction. We hereby recommend that His Majesty King Sacha of Pashia awards you with the King's Golden Medal of High Knowledge.'

Jamil stood there listening to the chairman in disbelief. He was so happy he could not even show it. He smiled and looked at the gallery where Haske was jumping and clapping with excitement. She raced down the stairs towards him and hugged him passionately. 'Well done. I'm so proud of you. I'm really impressed,' she started to cry as she hugged him again.

'I did it for you,' he whispered into her ears.

'I know and thank you.'

Haske took Jamil to the palace in her official car.

Queen Natasha broke royal protocol to welcome Jamil outside the huge doors with her usual smile. She was excited. 'Well done, my son,' she said and hugged him for the first time since he arrived in Pashiapolis. 'I'm really happy and proud of you,' she said ushering him into the dining room. 'So you are a golden boy too and not just a handsome face. You see, so many people fail this test. It's extraordinary you passed with distinction. This is out of this world. First attempt. Distinction!'

Haske slipped away, leaving Jamil and the queen alone at the dining table.

'You must be hungry,' Queen Natasha continued. 'I can see you've lost weight. We're not going to wait for the king today. Today is a special day and he'll understand.'

'It's all right. I'm so happy I passed it and will not be banished.'

'You must be very happy and proud. Now you have a medal to show your people when you return to the island. I hope you take the princess with you. She needs some exposure in life and you are the perfect person to provide it. She needs a bit of adventure and travelling to make her see and appreciate the world. That's why I'm so happy for both of you. You can return to your island a happy and proud person, and as someone who has been able to achieve something extraordinary.'

Jamil looked at Queen Natasha without saying a word.

'Honestly, I've a feeling you can do anything ... a feeling that with you everything is possible ... that you can shake mountains. I don't know why but I believe you can make the impossible possible. At fifteen you tricked the monster with your three-goat plan. Then you embarked on an adventure to retrieve the key. On the way, you experienced a shipwreck and later crossed the desert. You've overcome so many obstacles to get to Pashia and today you passed one of the most difficult tests in the kingdom. This is extraordinary. Well done!

'I'm very happy for my daughter too. She's been very worried. I must say that she's changed a lot since you came into her life. In Pashia we have a saying that a girl changes more than a dozen times before she becomes a woman. Since you came here, Princess Asia has changed from a girl to a woman. She has matured. She has blossomed. Bloomed. She's now a woman ready to take on life. You came into her life at the very right moment and I can see the two of you maturing together into a bright future. I want her to experience life and that's why I am willing to let her go with someone like you by her side to keep her safe.'

As her mother finished, Haske walked in looking majestic in new clothes. She was wearing a long red gown and high heels. She wore long shiny earrings and a diamond. 'At last there's something big to celebrate,' she said. 'I'm so happy. Today will go down as the happiest day of my life.' She studied herself carefully in one of the mirrors with delicate plaster carvings, then turned to Jamil. 'Jamil has shown the world what sort of brain he's got.'

Queen Natasha gave Jamil something to drink. 'She's gorgeous isn't she?' she whispered with a radiant smile. 'You are indeed a lucky boy.'

Haske walked closer. Jamil could smell her perfume. 'I'm so proud of you, Jamil. I'm so happy. Now you can dream of bigger things in life. This I hope is a big step towards the realisation of your dream.'

'Don't get carried away my little Princess. Only King Sacha knows what happens next. He decides and his decision in his kingdom is final,' Queen Natasha cautioned.

As they ate, King Sacha entered the dining room on crutches. He looked sad and Jamil felt something was not right. They stopped eating and stood while the king sat down. Jamil noticed that for the first time since they met, King Sacha avoided eye contact. Jamil looked at Haske who looked worried too. Queen Natasha asked nervously. 'Are you okay, my love?'

'No I'm not,' he replied.

They ate in silence.

'I've heard about you passing the first test,' King Sacha began, still not looking directly at Jamil. 'As you can see I'm not in good shape to present the medal to you.' There was a long pause. Then the king went on hurriedly, 'I've ordered that you face three chimeras within the next forty-eight hours. You'll be placed under house arrest between now and the fight so that you don't run away.' As he spoke Jamil looked at the king and his vision became blurred. He felt like screaming but he remained calm. 'You're going to be given the medal and the key if you successfully fight and defeat the chimeras. You chose to come here and get the key. You had so many chances to change your destiny but you didn't. There is a price for everything. Nothing comes easy and cheap. Good luck, Wonderboy.'

Queen Natasha was devastated. Haske broke down crying.

'But he has suffered enough ....' Queen Natasha protested.

'But not in my kingdom and not for the key. This is my kingdom and it's my duty to defend the imperial traditions. Let me remind you that I'm the King of Pashia and the Guardian of the Key.' As two guards escorted Jamil out of the dining room, he heard King Sacha say: 'This is my kingdom and no one challenges me here and goes free.'

'What really is a chimera?' Jamil asked a guard.

'A chimera can be half human and half animal. It can be made up of various parts of animals. You see, King Sacha has fifteen chimeras and they are all different. No two chimeras are identical. They all have different features of animals. The most popular chimera in the kingdom has got the head of a lion, the body of a rhino, hands of human beings and the legs of a horse.'

'Thanks,' Jamil said, somewhat embarrassed that he didn't even know what he was supposed to fight.

'Look,' the guard continued voluntarily. 'I can see that King Sacha has chosen the three you are supposed to fight. They are the top three. Actually you don't fight chimeras, they are supposed to kill you. They are the secret weapons of King Sacha. Weapons of last resort, some people call them. He's very fond of them and uses them to get rid of his enemies and they are also used to get rid of hardened criminals sentenced to death. He enjoys watching the chimeras devouring human beings.'

'I see, but I've done nothing wrong.'

'You think you've done nothing wrong but the king decides here.'

'So I'm not fighting them?'

'No. You're to be killed by them,' the guard explained bluntly.

'And I cannot see what they look like?'

'No you can't.'

'Has anyone ever killed a chimera?' Jamil asked.

'No. Years ago, a man escaped from the ring and ran away.'

Jamil laughed at himself in his cell. He wondered why he had never considered fighting the chimeras seriously. Perhaps it was because he had been thinking about Haske more than anything else. Even when the chimeras were mentioned in conversations, Jamil never bothered to pay attention to what was being said. He had the opportunity of seeing them with Haske who once jokingly threatened to throw him to the chimeras. Everyone knew they were kept in a secret place in the palace and brought out only on very rare occasions to devour human beings. It never crossed Jamil's mind that he would one day be in the ring with them. He never thought King Sacha would send him to such a violent death. 'After all, this would hurt the queen and the princess. So I must mean nothing to His Majesty,' thought Jamil. As he sat quietly in the cell, Jamil tried to form a mental picture of the animals. 'At least I saw the monster before I tricked it,' he thought bitterly.

'What's your last wish?' a guard asked Jamil.

'To see the princess before the fight.'

'She has asked for that already and King Sacha has agreed.'

The guard walked away and moments later came back. 'One last question, what do you want for your last supper?'

'Does it matter?'

'It does matter because it's your last supper.'

Jamil did not respond. That night, he slept well. When he awoke, it took some time for him to remember that this was to be his last day alive. The realisation did not make him nervous at all.

As he prepared for the fight, Jamil hid the piece of cloth Hakuri gave him in his clothes. 'This is so special to me. I might as well die with it,' he thought.

'Jamil,' a voice shouted. 'Prepare for your last journey.'

When he was ready, Jamil walked out of the cell and handed over his bag. 'That's all I've got.'

'That's the best way to die. As a brave man leaving no burden for anyone,' the guard said.

At the huge indoor stadium in the centre of Pashiapolis, Jamil was escorted into an underground cell. Even when the door was locked behind him, Jamil did not feel deep inside him that he was about to die.

About half-an-hour later, there was a knock and a guard walked in with Haske. She was smiling happily, and even winked at him. 'I've come to say goodbye. I've always admired your courage and will always remember you. You've taught me so many things. Be strong and have no fear. You've used your head so many times and it's time to use it again. It's yours to lose.' She turned to the guard. 'Could I have just one minute alone with him please?'

'You can have two minutes, Your Immaculate Highness Princess Asia of Pashia,' the guard courteously replied.

Haske gave him a small tin, the size of his thumb. 'Hide it somewhere,' she whispered.

He grabbed it and hid it with the cloth. 'What is it?'

'It's an ointment,' she said breathing heavily. Haske placed an earpiece into his right ear. 'I'll speak to you through the earpiece. Just follow my instructions. I know all the chimeras. I've seen them in action and know their weaknesses. Together we can defeat them,' she whispered looking straight into his eyes. 'Jamil! No fear, okay?'

'No fear,' he affirmed shaking her hands.

'Time up,' shouted a guard as the door opened.

'Good luck, wonderboy,' Haske said and walked away.

'She's right,' said the guard. 'You need lots of luck with the chimeras. They're the most vicious things I've ever seen. How does it feel to know you are about to die?'

Jamil did not answer.

Fifteen minutes later Jamil was escorted into the ring. He was not intimidated by the shouts and taunts. He tried to avoid looking at the crowd but wanted to see if he could catch a glimpse of Haske. From where he stood – just outside the ring, he could see her huge curly hair in the royal box. It appeared she was arguing with His Majesty King Sacha. He saw her storm out of the box in anger. Just as she disappeared from view, one of the guards told him to walk further. He looked up and could see himself on a huge screen with the words THE LAST WALK written underneath.

The master of ceremony entered the ring holding a microphone. The ring was big, about three times the size of a normal boxing ring. It was right in the middle of the brightly lit stadium. The master of ceremony made a call for silence. A guard brought the key and showed it to the crowd. 'His Majesty King Sacha of Pashia *May he rule over us for a long time* is Guardian of the Key and it is his responsibility to defend it by any means necessary. This young man here called Jamil has publicly challenged King Sacha by wanting the key. To carry out his royal duties, King Sacha has chosen three chimeras to defend the key. As you all know, the chimeras have never failed as the ultimate conquerors of human beings. No human being has ever defeated a chimera.

'As King Sacha always says "Human beings are by nature stupid. They play with fire and they get burnt."' The Master of Ceremony walked closer to Jamil. 'A stupid man is born every minute, one stupid young man has chosen to die and will die before our eyes. It is his choice. As you all know, King Sacha's philosophy is simple. Destiny is choice not chance. Jamil, for those who don't know, left the island of Tatasi and came all the way to get the key. He chose to be in this kingdom, he chose to be here today, dead tomorrow.'

There were chants and songs in the stadium. 'You'll be gone in a minute,' some chanted. Others shouted, 'Let us hear your last prayers.' Jamil was not concerned. He looked closely at the royal box and noticed Haske was still not there.

'Let him die! Let him die! Let him die!' There were more chants from the crowd.

As he stood there waiting to see a chimera for the first time,

Jamil heard a noise in his right ear. 'Jamil, this is your Haske here. Nod twice if you can hear me.' Haske's delightful voice was coming through the earpiece. Jamil remained calm and nodded twice. 'GREAT! We're in business and we can defeat the chimeras together. I know them very well as I played with them when they were young and long before they were trained to kill. I've seen them in action and know their weaknesses. Generally, don't get too close to any chimera. Beasts always remain beasts. You need full concentration. Nothing must distract your attention. You cannot afford to make one mistake. Just like with the monster, there's only one winner and no second chance! Can you hear me?'

Jamil nodded twice again.

'Great. Use your imagination as you did when you tricked the monster. Go into this battle with no fear at all. Be determined as ever. Believe in yourself and in your strength and ability to do the best. Victory and the key are yours my dearest. Can you hear me?'

Again Jamil nodded twice.

The master of ceremony walked up to Jamil. 'Are you ready?'

'Yes. Bring them on,' he answered confidently.

'Your Majesty King Sacha of Pashia *May you rule over us for a long time*, Your Immaculate Highness Princess Asia, distinguished ladies and gentlemen, the young man who challenged the chimeras says he is ready. Here are the rules of engagement:

'In the spirit of fairness, Jamil will fight only one chimera at a time. We believe in a fair play. Do you understand?'

'Yes,' Jamil nodded.

'It is agreed you'll be under sanctions,' the master of ceremony announced.

'What does that mean?' Jamil asked.

'No one is allowed to come and help even if you are under attack.'

'But the chimeras have handlers I was told,' Jamil tried to argue.

'You want the key not the chimeras.'

'Okay,' Jamil conceded.

'It's a fight to the finish with each chimera. No draws.'

'Agreed.'

'No running away from the ring.'

'Agreed.'

'JAMIL,' the master of ceremony's voice boomed through the hall. 'Are you ready?'

'YES!'

'First chimera please!' The master of ceremony walked out of the ring.

Haske's voice came through the earpiece: 'The fight has begun. Calm down. The first chimera is the one I call the Predator. It's got the head of an elephant without the long nose and tusks, the body of a gorilla and the legs of a horse. The Predator is very powerful and its strength lies in its ability to punch its victims to death. It's got a deadly accurate blow that everyone calls the Killer Blow. The Predator's main weapon is the gloves with spikes. Whatever you do please don't get too close and don't blink while fighting it. Don't worry I know its weakness. It's very easy to defeat.'

There were chants as the chimera walked slowly and arrogantly into the ring. The handlers restrained it from attacking Jamil. The chimera started to jump around the ring to the chants of the crowd. Jamil was invited to the centre of the ring. He stood there two-thirds the size of the chimera and for the first time he was genuinely scared. The chimera was huge, grunting and puffing anxiously. Its gorilla-body was covered in paint and it wore multicoloured shorts. Jamil surveyed the chimera from head to hoof. It had specially made hooves with springs designed to enable it to run, jump and strike its deadly blow. Jamil's heart almost stopped when the handlers removed the cloth covering the gloves. Each glove was bigger than his head and had a dozen or so shiny metal spikes protruding from them. A handler asked Jamil, 'Would you like to touch them?' Jamil did not answer and did not touch the shiny sharp spikes. 'They are non-lethal weapons, okay?' the handler said smiling.

'Don't be scared Jamil,' Haske's voice came through the earpiece. The bell rang signaling that the fight had started. 'Remember not to get too close, please.' Haske advised. 'It's got poor sight and can only attack at close range. Keep your distance. Walk around the edge, along the ropes. It hates attacking on the edge. Its area of attack is right in the middle of the ring and at high speed. Just slow it down and keep walking around the ring. It takes a while for it to strike its killer blow and has particular rituals it must go through.'

The chimera leaned on a rope then started running across the ring from one end to the other. Haske's voice spoke again: 'This is what is called rope-a-dope. Play the game with it and run in the opposite direction. It's getting ready to strike.' As the chimera began to run and increase its speed, so did the chants and cheers from the crowd. 'Two more runs and it'll deliver the killer blow. I'll blind it using an invisible laser beam now. It'll continue running but will be vulnerable to attack because it cannot see where it is going.' Jamil noticed the chimera was running aimlessly and at full speed. He stood and watched it. The handlers were anxious and shouting from the sides. 'Jamil,' Haske said anxiously, 'it is totally blind and this is the best time to bring it down. As it runs back and forth, trip it so that it can fall. It never rises when it falls.' Jamil waited for the right moment then applied a sliding tackle. The chimera fell on its spiked gloves and blood gushed out of its face. Jamil returned to his corner while the handlers rushed in and attended to the chimera. 'Well done. Well timed. Excellent move,' said Haske. There was panic in the ring as the chimera was dragged away.

'You cheated,' someone shouted from the edge of the ring.

'Give Jamil something to drink,' the master of ceremony said through the microphone.

'Jamil,' Haske's voice came through. 'Please, don't drink anything they give you. King Sacha has a plan B which is to poison you. Just concentrate on your next fight.'

Jamil sat and waited. He was happy that he had defeated the first chimera, something no one had ever done. He was happy that Haske was with him in this fight. Happy that something connected them even though no one could see it. He was happy and confident and could even smile at the ringside officials.

'Energy drink for you Jamil,' said a lady with a glass in her delicate hands. 'You need a lot of energy to fight the next chimera.'

'Don't fall for whatever she says,' Haske cautioned again. 'She's working for King Sacha. It's poison in there.'

Jamil politely declined the drink.

'Are you ready for the second chimera?' the master of ceremony asked.

'Yes.'

'Second chimera please,' he announced and remained in the ring.

As the second chimera emerged, the crowd screamed and shouted. Haske assured him. 'Don't be intimidated by the screams and shouts. This is the one I call the Vampire – it has the head of an eagle, the body of a goat and the legs of a kangaroo. Don't be deceived, it has wings and can fly. It can detach itself from the kangaroo legs at will and it has very deadly claws.'

Jamil fixed his anxious eyes on the chimera but could not help hearing shouts of 'NO FLY ZONE! NO FLY ZONE!' As he wondered what it was all about, Haske explained, 'The crowd wants an iron net put over the ring so as to stop you from flying away.' Jamil walked closer to the chimera. There were five handlers around it. He could see the shiney claws being polished. He locked eyes with the chimera for sometime. As they exchanged glances, Jamil noticed the handlers untie the wings and spray them with something. The chimera was shorter than Jamil.

The master of ceremony asked for silence. 'His Majesty King Sacha of Pashia, king of humans and king of beasts.'

The crowd shouted in unison: '*May he rule over us for a long long time.*'

The master of ceremony continued, 'The king has listened to the will of the people and has imposed a no-fly zone.'

There was a huge ovation and the crowds again shouted 'NO FLY ZONE! NO FLY ZONE!'

'Let's hear the drums of war,' shouted the master of ceremony.

A group of eight boys in uniform beating drums marched towards Jamil singing:

'You've nowhere to run
You've nowhere to hide
You've nowhere to fly
You're on your own
Jamil, you're on your own!'

'Jamil, the net is in place and the lights will be dimmed as there will be fireworks, something to entertain the crowd. Don't be scared. Have no fear. King Sacha imposed a no-fly zone because he thinks you can fly. He doesn't take chances at all. The vampire is one of the most destructive chimeras ever created. Its claws are tipped with explosives and it can attack any object either moving on the ground or flying. There is a no fly zone because it was created to attack from the ground up. While attacking, it begins its deadly ascent from the middle of the ring. To defeat it you need to lure it into a position it's comfortable with and then trick it. First go into your corner. Then just pretend that you are going to fly. That's a trick of course. Once it's locked onto you, it'll calculate the pace and fly upwards. Like an eagle, once it has locked onto something it cannot change direction midair. My plan for it is to attack the corner and burn itself there. Should we succeed, its dangerous claws will hit the wood on the edge of the ring and catch fire which in turn will burn the chimera. The chimera can release its explosives on humans but not on wood. Maximum alert and flexibility are required. Timing is essential. One second too early, you're gone. One second too late you're gone. You've got to get it right.'

Jamil and the Vampire exchanged nervous glances as they both paced around warming up. Jamil walked to his corner and sat on the second rope looking upwards as if he wanted to fly. 'That's good,' Haske said. 'Make it believe you are about to fly.'

The Vampire retreated to its corner and began to shake and jump. 'Jamil, it's on full frontal attack mode … get ready to be the target.' The crowd started cheering the Vampire, 'GO FOR HIM! GO FOR HIM!'

The Vampire opened its mouth and its wings within seconds

and lunged forward. As soon as it brought out its two clawed feet aiming the explosives directly at him, Jamil jumped down and rolled on the floor. The Vampire flew over him and went straight into the corner of the ring. As he rolled on the floor, Jamil could see fireworks and the Vampire flapping its wings and screaming desperately. The crowd was screaming too. The fireworks continued as the explosives caught fire upon impact with the corner of the ring. The Vampire began to burn in its own fire.

'Great stuff again Jamil! Well done. Perfect timing. Everybody expected you to go up and you went down. See how it's burning? Don't pity it. It could be you burning instead. Ask for a break.'

'Can I go to the toilet please?' Jamil asked the master of ceremony.

'Oh yes. Stay there until we call you.'

Jamil looked at the Vampire again. Its eyes were bulging as it screamed in pain, flapping its wings. The handlers were desperately trying to put out the fire.

'Just go and rest Jamil,' Haske implored. 'Let the Vampire burn in its own fire.'

Jamil was escorted to the toilet.

'Well done,' Haske's voice came through after a while. 'You've done what no one has ever done before, defeated two chimeras in a row.' Then there was a long silence. Then to Jamil's relief Haske's voice came through the earpiece again. 'You may not have seen it, but the Vampire has burnt to death in your corner. They're preparing the ring for the last chimera. I have also moved to a place close to the ring. If you still have the ointment, please rub it on both eyes now. Apply moderately. It'll take some time to work.' Jamil did as Haske ordered and hid the tin in his clothes again.

About half-an-hour later, a guard came and escorted Jamil to the ring. Haske spoke through the earpiece again: 'I can see you coming out but don't look for me. You are about to face the most dangerous animal ever created and the most dangerous weapon King Sacha has got in his arsenal. No fear Jamil, we'll defeat it together. Whatever you do don't panic. This chimera has the head of a lion with a single horn in the middle, the ears of an antelope, the body of a goat, and the long arms and legs of a human being. It's called the Magician.'

The crowd stood and cheered the Magician as it entered the ring with two handlers. 'Don't be intimidated by this one. Its strength is in its serpent's tail which at the moment is hidden from everyone. When it is ready, it'll bring it out and release a deadly poison on you which will numb you and make it easy for it to attack and devour you. Since you have the ointment in your eyes, you will see the serpent's tail when it emerges and see the poison when released. You'll be able to dodge it and survive. The Magician loses its power if the poison does not numb the prey. It cannot devour its prey unless it is poisoned. That's the only way it can create new poison,' whispered Haske. 'Jamil,' she continued, 'I can see the handlers giving it instructions to start with a fist fight. You have to fight this on a one-to-one basis I'm afraid. Good luck.'

Jamil composed himself and sized up the chimera.

'Jamil,' the master of ceremony shouted. 'Are you ready?'

'Yes, I am.'

'Do you want to say your last prayers?'

'God help us all.'

Haske warned him not to get too close to the chimera. 'It can also injure its prey in a face-to-face combat before it releases the poison,' she whispered. 'Avoid contact as much as possible. This chimera would like to wrestle you but don't. It bites and its teeth can be dangerous.'

Jamil started jumping around like a boxer.

The chimera immediately charged forward trying to grab Jamil with its long arms. Jamil avoided any contact. He fixed his eyes on the beast and when it stopped Jamil landed two blows on it. The chimera was startled. It shook its head and lunged forward. Jamil dodged and hit it as it went past.

'Great stuff!' shouted Haske. 'It did not expect a counterattack. Keep hitting it.'

Every so often the chimera would stop and roar and dance to the tune of a particular song being played in the stadium while the crowd chanted 'HAVE NO PITY! KILL HIM! KILL HIM!' Jamil avoided any close contact, running round the edge of the ring.

The Magician turned to Jamil and tried to grab him for a game of wrestling but Jamil successfully avoided him. Without any advance warning the Magician landed a deadly blow on Jamil. He fell and the crowd cheered. The Magician waited for him to stand up and landed another blow. Jamil was dazed and fell down again. Blood was now gushing out of his nose and mouth. The Magician started dancing in the middle of the ring. The crowd was pleased that Jamil was down and there were shouts of 'FINISH HIM! LET'S SEE THE MAGIC! MAGICIAN PLAY YOUR TRICKS!'

Jamil was in real pain now and as he tried to stand up and continue, the Magician kicked him. The chimera picked Jamil up and grabbed him by the neck. Jamil's eyes bulged and he screamed. The chimera seemed to enjoy it as it grabbed him tighter and tighter. When Jamil felt he could not breathe any longer, he closed his eyes. The chimera released its grip and drew him closer to its face. It stuck its tongue out as if to tease him. Jamil opened his eyes and could faintly see the wrinkled forehead of the lion's head. Still holding Jamil the Magician headbutted him three times and threw him out of the ring. There was huge applause in the stadium. The Magician continued to dance in the middle of the ring. Jamil could hear Haske's voice but didn't understand what she was saying. He lay on the ground in pain. He closed his eyes and for a moment he thought he saw Haske standing over him urging him to get up. Jamil thought he heard her say something like: 'You're down but not out! You can still defeat the Magician!' With a struggle he opened his eyes but she was not there. There were people around him shouting and screaming abuse at him.

'Throw him to the chimera,' shouted the master of ceremony. Some officials took Jamil from the floor and threw him into the ring. As the chimera advanced to hit him, Jamil managed to hit it first in its abdomen and stood up. The chimera was hurt. This move gave Jamil a few seconds to compose himself and continue to jump and hit the chimera. The two stood in the centre of the ring exchanging ferocious blows until the Magician stopped and ran to the rope dancing. There was more music and the audience sang and clapped.

'Now it is ready for the magic,' Haske told him. The lion's head with its antelope ears began to rotate slowly to the great applause of the crowd. 'Don't be fooled by this display,' Haske warned again. 'It's trying to divert your attention.' As the Magician turned and faced the crowd, still rotating its head and roaring, Haske's voice became nervous. 'It's entering its most dangerous phase now. Look closely and you'll see a serpent's tail emerge pointing at you. Can you see it?'

Jamil nodded.

'Have no fear. You can see what no one in the audience except the handlers and I can see. You can see the invisible weapon. You've got the third eye as we say here,' Haske said.

The Magician continued to entertain the crowd with its rotating head and roars. The serpent's tail was now out and aimed at Jamil. 'Once it is ready, the Magician will pause and spray you with the poison. It can see you even though it's facing the crowd. It's got an eye at the back of its head. So don't blink.' The Magician continued to jump around the ring, swinging its arms and transfixing the crowd with its rotating head and roaring. Jamil kept his eyes on the serpent's tail that had fully emerged. It was a multicoloured tail with a hole at the end. 'Once the colour changes to deep red, then the poison is ready to come out.' Jamil's eyes stayed on the tail. He noticed that the tail followed him wherever he went. 'It's now locked onto you, get ready to dive and roll.' Jamil's heartbeat raced as he noticed the Magician pause again, and this time the mouth of the serpent's tail opened and its colour changed. 'The poison will be released. Three, two, one – dive and roll,' instructed Haske. Jamil dived to the left and rolled as far as he could. 'Great stuff Jamil! You've done it again. Wonderful. If you can stand up and walk round then you have not been touched by the poison.' Jamil stood up and walked round looking at the dazed Magician and its handlers. The Magician had stopped entertaining the crowd and stood there looking at Jamil with real fright in its eyes. 'No one has ever dodged the poison before, that's why the Magician and its handlers are confused. They don't know what to do. Don't be scared. It has lost its magic. It's got no power left. It can only survive by devouring its prey and can only devour its prey if it has numbed it. You have broken the spell. It cannot do anything now but roar. It doesn't matter how long it lives, it's a dead chimera walking. One push and it'll fall down.' Jamil walked round the ring very proud of his victory. The crowd was confused. He decided to show convincingly that he had won by using one finger to push the Magician. The chimera staggered and fell. The crowd was shocked and bewildered. Jamil also could not believe his eyes. Haske jumped into the ring excited and agitated too. There was fear in her eyes. She urged the master of ceremony to hurry up.

The master of ceremony congratulated Jamil, calling him 'the boy who refused to be killed by the chimeras' and quickly handed over the key and the King's Gold Medal. As Jamil proudly showed them to the stunned crowd, Haske pulled him away. 'This way,' she started to run.

'Why the hurry, Haske?'

'Can't you see King Sacha is giving out orders up there?'

Jamil followed her through a network of tunnels, down the stairs and then to a metal door which she opened with difficulty. Haske jumped into a convertible car with the number plate HMKS 1. 'Let's go.'

'But this is King Sacha's favourite car,' said Jamil.

'Yes, jump in quickly,' she pleaded with fear in her eyes.

As she started to drive through the back streets of Pashiapolis, Jamil could still not understand why they were running away. 'But I won, why are we running away?'

'It's one thing to win, it's another thing to get out of Pashiapolis alive,' Haske explained driving very fast through the back streets. She almost knocked down some pedestrians as she turned into a junction and sped on the highway. 'The easy bit is done, now the hard bit starts,' Haske said still looking very anxious.

'You mean fighting the chimeras was easy?'

'Okay, you've done half the job. Now it's my turn to do the other half.'

'What do you mean?'

'King Sacha has plans just in case you won.'

'Like what?'

'He has positioned assassination squads in different parts of the stadium and town. I know where they are and have so far avoided them.'

'Assassins?'

'King Sacha is the Guardian of the Golden Key and I'm his only daughter. These are two things he'll never let go.'

'And I'm taking both away from him. It's winner takes all in Pashiapolis. He wanted to make life difficult for me, didn't he?'

'Don't talk too much. King Sacha never leaves things to chance. We don't know what he's got planned ahead.' After a pause Haske added. 'Queen Natasha was secretly wishing us well in our plans. She'd be very happy if we manage to get out of this place alive.'

'How I wish I could let her know that we are safe and thank her for her support.'

'We'll do that in a minute.'

'How?' a puzzled Jamil asked.

'This car has a video link with the Queen. Remember this is King Sacha's favourite car.'

'HMKS1 – His Majesty King Sacha Number 1' Jamil said laughing.

'Hey look,' Haske shouted when she spotted three assault helicopters chasing them. 'Just in time,' she said as they reached a forest and turned into it. 'I know this area very well. Queen Natasha's garden is up there and the forest is very dense. The helicopters can't shoot at us.' They drove for about an hour in the dense forest and Haske began to relax the farther they drove away from Pashiapolis.

'Now we can talk to Queen Natasha' she said with a big smile. She stopped the car and pressed a button on the dashboard. A mini video screen appeared and after a brief moment they saw the smiling face of Queen Natasha. 'Mummy, just to let you know that we are safe and out of Pashiapolis.'

'Great. Congrats. His Majesty is very angry. Please take care and safe journey. I love you all. Wonderboy, please take good care of my daughter.'

'I will and thank you for everything.'

The reception was interrupted.

'Let's get out and walk the rest,' Jamil suggested.

'Why?'

'I have a feeling it will be safer. You said King Sacha doesn't leave anything to chance. He may know exactly where we are from the conversation with Queen Natasha.'

'Quick thinking,' said Haske smiling and rummaging in the bag on her lap. 'Here' she said giving him new clothes, a wig, and a fake moustache to dress himself up.

'You've got everything well thought out.'

'Never take anything for granted with King Sacha. I know what the key means to you. As for me, I want to have an adventure too …'

They continued on foot.

From afar they saw a van approaching from the opposite direction and ran into the bushes and hid. 'Good idea to abandon the car earlier,' Haske said as they hid.

Armed soldiers were now on foot combing the area. Jamil and Haske climbed up a tree and hid. When they passed Jamil waited for a long time before he came down and surveyed the area. When he was sure they were alone, he helped Haske down.

They decided to continue through the dense forest towards the river where Haske had a getaway boat moored.

They walked in total silence. When they got to the river, Jamil surveyed the whole area carefully before signalling to Haske to jump into the boat.

'The next town is The Den and if we are not caught we should be there at dawn. We'll sail in total darkness,' Haske whispered.

'Just when I thought the adventure was over …'

'Maybe yours, but mine has only begun.'

The sun was setting as the two sat in the boat. The rays of the sun reflected on their exhausted and exhilarated faces as they sat and looked at each other in silence and disbelief. Jamil noticed Haske was crying. He comforted her. After a while she broke the silence.

'What are you thinking about?' Haske asked.

'Many things.'

'Like what?'

'Like my journey, my life and how I got to where I am now and the things and people that helped me.'

'For example?'

'So many people helped me. The old man in the Land of Mourners. I'll always remember Hakuri in The Den. I will introduce you to her as I promised to see her again.' He paused. 'You helped me, and Queen Natasha.'

'What about the things?'

'My pet goat Lucky, the parrot and owl in The Den and the ointment you gave me … oh, and yes, before I forget it,' he stood up and brought out the piece of cloth from his clothes. 'This is what Hakuri gave me.'

Haske screamed and almost fell into the river. Jamil grabbed her.

'What's wrong?'

Haske started to cry. 'It's nothing to do with you,' she assured Jamil.

She opened her bag and brought out the other half of the hand-woven cloth.

'This is incredible,' Jamil said shaking his head. 'So Hakuri is your grandmother. I should have guessed but she thought you were dead.'

'I always knew there was something that attached us. I don't know anything about her.'

The two sat there looking at each other as if meeting for the first time. Both seemed shaken by the discovery.

Their boat sailed away from Pashia Kingdom.

EPILOGUE

Jamil and Haske escaped from Pashia Kingdom. In The Den, Jamil showed Haske where he had worked as a grocer. Kolo told him that Hakuri was very ill and had returned to Rasmarat to rest for good. 'If you want to see her alive, you'd better hurry.' Jamil took the owl and the parrot and hastened to Rasmarat with Haske. There he was told Hakuri had gone to her ancestral village of Kerenia. They continued and found Hakuri on her deathbed.

'Ming,' Hakuri whispered in a barely audible voice with eyes closed. 'I knew you'd come. I was waiting for you. Someone like you does not make a promise and not fulfil it. I knew you'd succeed in Pashia Kingdom. I'm happy you were able to get the key and in the process humiliated King Sacha. Above all, I'm grateful you liberated my beloved grandaughter Wintana. There was a reason I gave you the piece of cloth. This is your *sudba*, your destiny. I don't know how many more days I have now that I have seen you and my grandaughter. I'm ready to go now. I've forgiven everyone including King Sacha. There is a reason why I gave you the name Ming, the one who was born under lucky stars, the traveller who reaches his destination. But listen to me Ming, you're not there yet. You're still on the journey. One thing I must tell you is that you will at some point in the future receive a call to return to the island. Something inside you will tell you when the time comes. Don't ignore it. Return with the key immediately. There is a reason why you succeeded in getting it.'

Two days later, Hakuri passed away in her sleep.

Jamil and Haske returned to Rasmarat where Haske's mother lived with her family. Jamil and Haske remained in the city for over a decade until one night Jamil had a strange dream and thought it was time to return to the island. He and Haske booked their flight to Pearl Islands as Tatasi was now called.

THE END

Lightning Source UK Ltd.
Milton Keynes UK
UKOW01f0508300617

304366UK00001B/7/P